Tamarack

The Beekeepers Daughter

A novel by
Peggy Poe Stern

Moody Valley
Boone, North Carolina

Published by
Moody Valley Publishers
475 Church Hollow Road
Boone, N.C. 28607
moodyvalley@skybest.com

Although its seed germinated from an actual trial case, this is a work of fiction. Names, characters, places, and incidents either are the product of the author's imagination or are used fictitiously. Any resemblance to actual persons living or dead, events or locales is entirely coincidental.

Cover painting by Peggy Poe Stern

Library of Congress Control Number. 2003115096

ISBN: 1-59513-054-3

Printed by Moody Valley

Printed in the United States of America

November 2005

Comments made to the author about
"Tamarack."

"You know, this would make a great movie. 'Deliverance' did."

"I swear it left a touch of vinegar in my blood and an ache in my soul."

"I couldn't put it down, but, well, I don't know."

"I read it at one sitting and hated every minute of it. Why didn't you make it a longer book? I wanted to read more."

"My husband was home sick, and he thought I was coming down with a stomach complaint. It aggravated him to see me sit and read, so I had to read it in the bathroom. My poor bottom stayed numb from that wooden seat."

"Now, I have to tell you this. There were four or five words I didn't like a tall. You know, you ought to stop all this other stuff you're doing and write all the time."

"What did others think? I thought it was rough around the edges."

"I knew there was something I didn't like about men. You just told me what."

"Don't you think it's a little harsh for just anybody to read?"

"It left my mind vibrating. I've not figured out what to think about it."

"I didn't like it. When are you going to write another one?"

"My husband wants to read it after I'm finished, but I might give it back to the woman I borrowed it from."

"Do you have any more of those books printed up? I need to buy one for my sister and one for me. I loaned the one I had to all my neighbors and they wore it out."

"You mean the preacher actually came to your house and got one? Did you charge him for it?"

"Dad burn your mangy hide. You kept me awake most all night."

"Confound you! You kept me awake 'til four o'clock this morning and I have to be up by six."

"There may be some people that don't believe such people exist, but in my job, I work with them every day."

"I don't care if that book is just a galley copy for your own purpose. You've got it in your hand and I want to buy it."

"Do I have to pay you for it? Can I read it first? If I read it, then brought it back, you could sell it to somebody else and they wouldn't know it."

"Did all this happen to you?"

"Where do you buy something like this from?"

"Aren't you afraid you'll make somebody mad, talking about them like that?"

"Well, good luck to you. I just don't know if people will pay to read stuff like this."

"Honey, why don't you write a nice sweet love story that everyone will enjoy?"

"I hate this other book you're writing. It might be a love story, but it don't have the fire and passion Tamarack does!"

"I came to buy that book I heard you wrote. I want to see how you did it. If you wrote one, I know I can. I'm a lot bigger than you."

"The second time I read it, I started to understand."

"Oh, thank you for not writing that scene more explicit. I don't think I could have stood it."

Dedicated to:

Bill Kaiser:
Thank you for beliving...

Special Thanks to:

Bart and Caroline Bare: for taking the time and care to edit this novel.

Mari-Lis Smyth: a whiz at editing.

Chloe Coleman: who keeps an eye on plants and seasons.

Doug Kaiser: for taking cover pictures.

David Lee Kirkland: from Missouri, who spent many hours reviewing my writing.

To Dave Shook: neighbor and friend who gave information in the year 1992.

Red Lyons: for his assistance

Dianne Cornett Deal: who assisted with research.

Written comments on
"Tamarack"

"Tamarack touched me in a place I didn't know I had."
Ree Strawser, author of "Long Gauze Dress"

"This is your best writing."
John P. McAfee, author of "Long Walk in a Sad Rain" and "On Rims of Empty Moons"

"It is an important book. Many will thank you for writing it. Keep it up."
Grace Wakeman

"Tamarack was just as hard to put down (as Heaven High and Hell Deep). I've read thousands of books, and as you well know, not every writer can seize the reader's interest and <u>hold</u> it to the very end. You are a born story teller – it's a true gift that you have."
Elizabeth McAfee, Artist

"Occasionally borders on brilliant."
David Lee Kirkland

Part One

Beyond Endurance

1991

Chapter 1

The sun shines on Tamarack Mountain, sometimes it shines while it rains. In the spring, the air is sweet with Locust blossoms. In the summer, Sourwood trees have clusters of blooms hanging longer than a man's hand.

Tamarack has everything a honeybee could want, and Jay Press knows it. There are seventy-two stands of bees semi-circling his pine slab house. He built each stand, each bee gum, himself.

Bees have given him income for sixty years. He got his first bee gum at the age of twenty, a year after he got married.

Made him mad to think about marrying Ivy.

Jay felt the warmth of the sun on his shock of white hair. A breeze touched his beard and shook a crumb of cornbread loose. He stuck his hand into the pocket of his faded blue work pants. The pocket part had been gone for years. Worn clean through. He adjusted his crotch, lingering to fondle a while. He felt a twinge, a tickle of pleasure, then it was gone, lost like youth.

Bees buzzed by him busy doing their job. His hand stopped its movement as his eyes watched the bees. Some things didn't change. Bees didn't. Folks' love of the sweet, golden stuff didn't. Them summer folks paid good money for a quart of honey so long as they got to gawk at a shabby old man, a dilapidated house, and a bunch of bees filling the air.

Summer folks, they came. They bought a single jar, or they filled their cars with cases. Every jar had to have a label, the one with the picture of him wearing a long beard of bees. The picture had been on the front page of the local newspaper. *Carolina Farmer* and *Blue Ridge Electric* ran the picture in their magazines. One did an article on him. It more than doubled his business.

It was high time he was recognized. Important! That's what he had become. Reckon that would show Ivy she shouldn't have left him.

He took his hand from his pocket and walked through the weeds leading from the bee gums to the front of his house. He heard a vehicle grinding its way up the steep incline. It took a little climbing to get up Tamarack.

Summer folks were coming early this year. The thought left a bad taste in his mouth.

They came earlier each year, he decided. Greedy asses. Wanting more and more stuff, like honey and land and the good life mountain folks had. Soon there wouldn't be a scrap of ground left for normal folks like him. Hell, there wouldn't be a sourwood or Locust left for a bee to suck its bloom.

Jay grinned. He'd just add a dollar to the price. They wouldn't climb all the way up Tamarack and not buy at least one jar.

He saw the car take the long curve down the road a piece. It was oxidation blue with rusty fenders that rattled. This wasn't summer folks. Whoever was driving this car was poor as spider piss.

He wouldn't get a blame thing outta this aggravation. Jay leaned against the corner of the house and waited.

The car pulled into the yard, mashing grass that was trying to grow. The man behind the wheel didn't cut the engine off while a woman got out. Instead, he backed up and took off fast. It appeared the man thought leaving Tamarack was preferable than coming to it. The faster he left the better.

"What tha hell?" Jay mumbled as he glared at her.

The woman saw him and walked toward him— slow. Her first steps were hesitant then determined. Her dress hung about her body. Her feet were clad in shoes run over at the heels. The bones in her shoulders stuck up. Loose skin wrinkled her throat and puckered her face. A sharp, slightly hooked nose, pointed at him. Her eyes, the blue of a Tamarack sky, watched him hard with determination and something more.

His jawbones clenched, teeth grinding. Hell, if it wasn't her. It was Ivy. Just like she looked the day she run off. Damn her. She was on his land again. She wouldn't leave him this time. She was his now, all his.

She came on and stopped just out of his reach. She watched him closely. He had gotten older, and grayer, and dirtier. Tobacco still stained his beard. Food still clung to the hairs. He still smelled. The look in his eyes made a quiver go from her toes to the top of her head. Her hair lifted by its roots—just like always.

"Hello Pa. Don't you have a civil greeting for your daughter?" she watched as his eyes clouded, puzzled, uncertain, then cleared.

"Beulah Dean," he said. "It's been a long spell."

"No Pa. It ain't Beulah Dean. It's me, Mary. Your oldest. Remember?"

His eyes narrowed. His jaw reclenched. He remembered. "Whatta ye want?"

"Want you to wish me happy birthday, Pa. I'm sixty years of age today. Can't believe it can you? Ain't set eyes on you or this place for forty- three years."

"Yer the spittin' image of yore maw. Same smart mouth too. Thought you were her when I first laid eyes on ye."

"Smarter than ma. I left quicker than she did," Mary said.

He straightened. His hands went into both pockets.

"Who brought ye?"

"Doug. Remember Tobe? The man I married. Doug's his brother."

"Where's Tobe?"

"Don't know. Left him for good, I did. Three days ago."

"Yer not stayin' here."

"Don't intend to. Just came so you could wish me happy birthday. Remember sixty years ago? Remember that tiny girl-child Ivy birthed on the kitchen floor? You were out with the bees. Didn't help her none."

He spat a stream of ambeer on the ground between her feet. It left brown specks on white skin. She didn't move.

"Has either of my sisters come back to see you? Reckon not. Outta the four of us I thought one might have visited afore me. Wished they had. Coulda saved me a long trip if one of 'em had the guts to come back."

She looked around the place remembering his picture in the newspaper. None of the money he got from honey had been spent on fixing the place up. He was so tight his ass squeaked when he walked. Somewhere around here he had most every dollar he ever got hold of.

"Just like Ivy. Both of ye had tha devil in ye. Neither worth killin. It's what ought ta been done to the both of ye long ago. Fool not ta done it."

"Fool. It's the right word," she took a step back then moved out into the weedy yard. She saw straggling flowers her ma planted over sixty years ago. Funny how something could live that long uncared for and unwanted.

He moved toward her. She saw his legs were still strong in their step. Age hadn't bent his back or crippled his muscles. He always reminded her of poison ivy. You couldn't kill out the stuff. Once it got on you, you broke out all over and suffered the torment. Only time could heal the oozing blisters of poison ivy. Sometimes it left the skin scarred.

He took another step toward her. She turned to face him and he stopped.

"Ma's still alive. I guess you know that. Ma is almost as old as you, and she's still living. Life is funny that away," Mary said as she looked beyond the bee gums to the woods. "Life don't hold no justice unless you take the trouble to make it that away."

She remembered playing in the woods as a kid, pretending to be somebody else, somewhere else. She had wanted to be happy. Tried to laugh a time or two. He always found her. Always stopped her happiness. He said laughter was the devil's making. Women came from the devil. Tempted by a snake they were. Needed their heads bruised. The Bible said so.

He quoted the Bible but never read it. Couldn't read. Wouldn't go to church. Wouldn't let any of them go. Words of the Bible changed sometimes, all depending.

She could read. She went to school some, sat in the back corner pretending to be invisible. Didn't want the kids looking at her. They would know.

The teacher knew, and she wouldn't look at her. Looked beyond her and never called on her for anything. One Christmas, the teacher gave her a plastic comb. She hid it in the corncrib and used it when she wanted to be somebody else. It disappeared. Beulah Dean must have stolen it, probably still had her plastic comb.

Hattie could have taken it. Hattie wasn't right in the head. She heard things that weren't there, saw things nobody else could see.

Right strange it was. Pa said it made his skin crawl. He stayed away from Hattie the most. He slapped her the most when she was close enough for him to hit.

Then there was Carrie. She was the baby. Whenever Pa started to climb the ladder to the loft, she would whisper, "Hide me, Mary. Hide me." She ran away when she was thirteen. Married a man that was fifty-six years old.

She turned from the woods and looked at the house. Boards hung crooked. Pieces of rusted tin roof were flapping with the breeze. The tin in the far right corner was gone completely.

That was her place in the attic. The little corner she had slept in—an inescapable hellhole.

"Ivy never deserved to live. That woman. A thorn in a man's side. Nothing but torment to a man!" he spat again, a brown arch that traveled beyond her.

"Nobody deserved to live like that. Ma certainly didn't. Nothing does," Mary said.

Her hand touched her dress pocket, then she rubbed her hand down the side of her dress as though she wanted to get the wrinkles out, but the wrinkles stayed where they were. Three days of wrinkles and wear. She had left Tobe with what she wore. She had left Tamarack when she was seventeen wearing a feed sack dress with no shoes.

She came back just a little better.

"You still got your mind? Not got that old timers disease or nothing?"

"Allus had my mind about me. It was Ivy. Brains made of corn mush," his eyes narrowed. His lips tightened underneath stained beard. "All damned girls she bore me. All like their maw."

"You deserved boys. All of 'em big mean brutes. All like you," she said. "All of 'em loving their ma."

He nodded as though it was a compliment. "Damned truth!" he said.

"Should never have been girls," Mary whispered. "Nary a one." She licked dry lips and felt a shiver go over her body. "See that little spot there? Where the roof is gone? That's where I slept. Remember?"

"Don't care where you slept."

"Yeah you did. You cared a lot." She told him, ignoring the anger in his words without looking at him. She was still looking at the missing tin on the roof. "Sound stills wakes me up most ever night— sound of that little girl crying. Causes pain. Too much pain to bear. It never ends. Reckon it never will. Wish to God it would. Won't. I know it now, after fifty-four years. It won't end."

"Fool! Goin on just like yore ma," he said and his jaw muscles twitched.

"Yeah. You're right there. Fool, just like Ma. Like all women at times. Fools." She winced and her eyes took on a far away look. "I'm hearing the little girl now. Her cries keep roaring between my ears. Sets my teeth on edge. Those cries continue to twist and wiggle in me like a belly full of worms. Won't go away; won't leave me be. Torment. Just pure torment."

"Ivy straight out. Off in the head's what ye are," he took his hands from his pocket and looked at his clenched fists. He swallowed this time instead of spitting.

She watched him. "Best year of my life was when they sent me away to that reform school. Tough bunch, where they sent me. I have to admit you taught me one thing. How to hurt another person. I could hurt 'em bad. They left me alone after a while. After they found out I would get even. You taught me that too, always get even."

His eyes narrowed.

She ignored the narrowing and said, "Remember that night? That first time? Pitch black it was. Blacker than hell. Couldn't see a thing. Didn't know it was you at first. Thought some kind of monster had me there on my pallet. Remember that pallet? Ma filled a feed sack full of pine needles for me to sleep on, just a little pallet, right size for a six-year-old. Those needles pricked my skin at times, but the needles smelled so good. I could roll over and the scent would rise around me. Made me feel safe, for a while. Made me feel like Ma loved and cared for me special." She swallowed. "You were such a big man. My face buried in the top of your belly. My legs were short but they spread off the pallet.

There were splinters in my feet from kicking the rough planks of the loft floor. Some got infected. Ma picked 'em out with her sewing needle," she swallowed again. "The pain! Dear God, the pain! I wanted to die, prayed to die. Didn't think I could live through it. Wanted to die bad, but I didn't. Pain don't kill. It goes on forever, but it don't kill."

She saw his fists clench, unclench. His eyes were round and beady. Snake eyes. Cold, unfeeling, waiting, watching, paralyzing.

She couldn't stop talking, had to continue. "Remember that big oak tree in the woods? You caught me there. Nearly beat the life outta me cause I tried to outrun you. Ma found me there, toted me all the way to the creek. She washed me up and done the best she could. Didn't die that time neither. Don't got no kids. Barren I am and allus will be. Doctor said it was scar tissue. Wanted to know how I got that away. I told him, born that way I reckon, but he knowd I lied. Didn't ask no more. Doctors don't want to know nothing. Nobody does. They let it happen. On an on an on. They don't care. They just let it happen."

She turned and looked him in the eyes. She had looked in them before. Hated them. Wanted to prick them blind with crabapple thorns.

She saw the pile of split wood beside the house where it had always been stacked. The axe was sunk into an upturned stump. The same stump? The same axe, she wondered, or had they been replaced? She used to think about that axe and what she wanted to do with it. One finger. One toe. One piece of nose. One hit in the belly. A slush sound like a hog being chopped in the throat as the blood rushed to get out. Yes, again, she thought of that.

Through a missing plank of underpinning, she saw a couple of mangy dogs lying under the house in the shade. Poor, half-starved things. They couldn't lap honey or eat bees. Must be enough rabbits to keep them alive. Hell of a life! Pure hell!

Mary saw him move. He was getting tired of standing, watching her, listening to her. She knew. She knew him.

"What tha hell ye here fur? Ye're after something, allus was, allus will be." He inclined his head toward the dirt road. "That feller left ye, so ye best get at walkin' while ye still can. Don't want the likes of you around here. Troublemaker is what ye are. You and Ivy alike. Don't never come back here no more."

She ran a shaky hand down her dress again. The hand buried in a fold, a pocket. Her mouth moved like she wanted to grin, instead she said, "I come to have a last look at the meanest son-of-a-bitch that ever lived. The no-account bastard that dared call himself a Pa." She didn't even see a flicker of his eyes.

He struck fast. His weight took her down in the dirt of the yard as his hands found her throat. His fingers dug and squeezed, bruising tender flesh and scraping up slivers of skin under his fingernails.

For a moment she was consumed with fear, the same fear that held her fast as a child. She was hearing the little girl cry, feeling her pain. Then, her mind came to her and cleared. She lifted her hand a fraction in her pocket and squeezed the trigger of her pistol. Noise of the shot rang in her ears. His hands lost strength but did not stop their choking.

She saw the wart below his left eye. The one she watched so many times before; the one with the long, ugly hairs. She eased the pistol from her dress pocket and pointed it at the wart. She squeezed. The wart was gone. Sunk into a hole no bigger than her finger. The hole tried to close a little just before the blood started to run. She had an urge to put the pad of her finger over the hole just to see if the blood would stop. She didn't.

She lay there for a little longer. Dead weight got heavy. She wiggled herself free.

Chapter 2

Folks called him Big Red. One of the best sheriffs the county ever had. He was tough. He was determined, and he was capable. He had a heart that could hurt, and a mind that could understand.

Big Red was the first on the scene.

She was sitting on the ground with his head in her lap. Big Red knew the man was dead. Part of his head was missing. Drying blood was on her dress, her hands. Her head was bowed, face wet with tears and streaked with dirt and blood.

She reminded Big Red of a child that had cried her soul out and could cry no more. Spasmodic sobs shook her body. Her head jerked like her neck was too weak to hold up the weight.

Big Red looked at her neck. It looked raw. Bruising was starting to appear and scratches had welted up. He saw the pistol lying in the dirt within her easy reach, took the toe of his boot and kicked it away from her. He nodded toward one of his deputies indicating he take it in as evidence.

He watched as his deputy opened a plastic bag and flipped the gun into it with a stick that had been lying on the ground. The deputy then took a pen out of his pocket and wrote on the plastic bag. Big Red almost grinned. The deputies were taught to use the pen to maneuver the weapon into a bag in order to protect fingerprints. He guessed a stick worked just as well.

He kneeled down beside the woman.

"What's your name?" Big Red's voice was compassionate.

"Mary."

"Mary what?"

"Tate."

"Mary Tate. Who's he?"

"Pa."

"What's his name?"

"Jay Press."

"You're Mary Press Tate?"

Her head nodded slightly. She had never looked at any of them. Her eyes remained on the face of her pa.

"Who shot him?" Big Red asked with a gentle voice.

"Me."

"You shot your father?" Big Red lifted his brows and watched her closely.

Her head nodded again.

"Why?"

"He aimed to kill me."

"Why did he want to kill you?"

She didn't answer.

"Your throat?" Big Red saw the purple-red of broken capillaries and knew what had happened.

"He choked me. Said after he kilt me he aimed to cut me up with the axe and feed me to the dogs."

"Why?"

"They're hungry."

Big Red frowned. "Can I help you stand up?"

She shook her head.

"Can you get up on your own?"

"No."

"Why not?"

"I'm watchin' him."

"Why?"

"He ain't dead," she whispered the words.

"Yes he is."

She shook her head again. "You can't kill poison ivy."

Big Red and the first deputy exchanged glances. Big Red stood up. The second deputy didn't move. He was busy taking down notes on a pad.

"Shock?" The first deputy questioned Big Red. "Probably."

"Should I get her up?" The first deputy asked.

"No. The ambulance will be here shortly." Big Red believed in letting people have their time, but he wanted more answers.

"Who does the gun belong to?" Big Red asked as he looked down on her.

"Me."

"Did you bring it here to shoot him with?"

"No."

"Why did you have it?"

"Protection."

"From whom?" Big Red saw her mouth tighten and her body seemed to shrink in on itself until she looked like a dried-apple doll, old and shriveled. "Protection from your pa?"

"No."

"Who then?"

She refused to answer.

"Who called for assistance?" Big Red asked her.

"Me," she lifted a trembling hand and cautiously touched the bullet hole below his eye. She jerked her hand away. "It's such a little hole. It shouldn't hurt much."

"He's dead." Big Red told her, but he didn't tell her the entire back of his head was missing. Nor did he tell her brain matter was smeared all over her lap.

She dug her hands into the dirt by her side, her fingers opening and closing spasmodically. "No he's not. See there. Blood looks worse than tobacco stain on his beard. Bees'll sting him now. They don't like the smell of blood."

Big Red looked at the bloodstains on the bushy beard. It was a small trickle drying brown, just a little of the red color was left. He had been dead a while.

"You left him to call for help then came back out here and put his head in your lap?"

She let a breath of air out her mouth and closed her eyes. "Dialed the O. Woman said she'd send the sheriff and ambulance. Didn't know what else to do. Thought he needed help. I didn't know what else to do," she repeated.

Fresh tears dripped off her jawbones. She looked too frail to hold up her head any longer. Her chin slowly went down until it rested on a chest of skin and bone. Big Red felt compassion, regret.

The siren of the ambulance could be heard at the bottom of the mountain as it started to climb up Tamarack. Big Red got tired of hearing the sound of that siren, mournful, telling of disaster. The sound was like an alarm clock waking him before he was ready to wake.

He turned to his deputy. "Read her rights, and book her for second degree murder."

"Can she get out on bail?" The deputy wondered out loud.

She lifted her head for the first time and looked at the deputy.

"You're gonna put me in a hay baler? I don't wanna be put through a hay bailer."

"There's no hay baler," Big Red said. "You won't be put through one."

She seemed relieved, looked back down at her pa and words eased out of her mouth in a sweet, small voice. "She's crying again. Bless her little heart, guess she don't know he can't hurt her no more."

"What are you talking about?" Big Red asked her gently.

"Pain," she said. "It ought to stop now."

"Are you in pain?" he asked.

"Not me."

"Does your throat hurt? Are you injured anywhere else?"

"I don't know."

"The ambulance is here. They'll take you to the hospital and have you checked out."

"Home," she said. "Should of had one. Couldn't a found me there."

"Who couldn't?"

"Devil," she said. "Wouldn't leave me be."

"Who's the Devil, Mary?" Big Red wanted to know.

She looked at her pa. "Once poison ivy gets on you, there's nothing you can do."

The ambulance pulled in behind the police cars and turned off the siren. The red light was still circling and flashing; reflecting off Mary and her pa. Two men and a woman hurried across the yard.

"He's already gone," Big Red told them. "Better check her throat before you take her to the hospital. I'll have a deputy ride in the ambulance with her. She's under arrest for murder."

Big Red stayed on after everyone else was gone. He had watched as evidence was collected and the job was done according to the book. There was nothing he could find fault with. Still, something lingered, troubled his senses. His gut told him to check and recheck. They had missed something. He was missing something. He walked around the site looking at the marked outline of the old man's body. It seemed the very air was trying to tell him something, but what?

He saw where blood had soaked into the ground from the belly wound, a lot of blood. That wound hadn't killed him. His heart had still been pumping the blood from his body. It would have been fatal given a little more time, but it was the face wound, the one that took the back of his head off, that took him out.

He bent over and observed the old man's and the woman's foot prints mashed in the weeds and grass. He saw where both of them had been on the ground, kicking up turf and dirt. From there, he tracked her steps through the yard straight into the house. He saw a couple smudges of blood on the floor. Another smudge of blood was on the edge of the table where the phone was. He looked at the phone. There was a dirt smudge. He had noticed how her hands clawed at the ground, digging up the soil, dirtying her hands as though she didn't realize what she was doing. All these things had been noted before. He wasn't seeing anything his men hadn't already seen. Why was he sure he was missing something? What wasn't right?

Chapter 3

Tobias Tate was a tub of a man. He was short, low to the ground and large around. His face was the ruddy color of a sunburned peach just before it rotted. His thinning hair was a corn shuck yellow heavy with gray.

Big Red knew Tobias wasn't a bit pleased when he showed up at his trailer door. In his youth, Tobias had his share of nicks with the law.

"What you want?" Tobias demanded.

"I came to have a talk with you Mr. Tate. It's important. It's about your wife."

"She ain't here."

"I know where she is. I thought you might want to know."

Tobe looked confused, hesitated then stepped back from the door to let Big Red come inside the trailer. The furnishings gave off a worn yard-sale appearance. But the place had been swept not long ago. Big Red could see broom marks in the dust on the floor.

Tobe did not ask him to sit, so he stood. His head was almost touching the ceiling of the trailer.

"Well, where is she?"

"Dorthea Dix Hospital in Raleigh."

"Wha-at?" His eyes widened. "Why? Was she in a car wreck or something?"

"It's a mental hospital. She's in for evaluation. You see, Mr. Tate, your wife shot her father."

Tobe moved the few steps it took to cross the room and sank down on the couch. He face became blank as he looked at Big Red.

"Shot him dead?" Tobe asked.

"As a doornail," Big Red added.

Puzzlement replaced the blank look. "He had to be older than the hills. Why would she shoot him? He'd die of old age before long."

Big Red pulled out a chair from the kitchen table and sat down even without an invitation. He took his note pad from his pocket and wrote the date with an ink pen. "I need a few answers from you if you don't mind."

"You aim to help her don't you?"

"That's why I'm here. Why did she leave you?"

Tobias squirmed and the couch sagged. "Craziness," he said, " just craziness."

"What kind of craziness?"

"She hadn't been doing too good lately. You see, sometimes she got these crazy things in her head. Things that didn't make no sense. Like, a few months back, she got this notion she was being witched."

Big Red's eyes narrowed as he looked at Tobe. Was this little tuber shooting him a line of bull? "Witched?"

Tobias hung his head and looked on the floor between his feet, shook his head and frowned. "You know those devil worshipers and all." He seemed hesitant to say anymore.

"What devil worshipers?"

"Foolishness. Just foolishness."

"Tell me about this foolishness. I have to know the truth if I'm going to help your wife."

Tobias's face crunched up like he knew better than that. "No law was ever out to help people. You and I both know that for a truth. She's up for murder, you say?" Tobias watched Big Red with distrust and dislike.

"Second degree." Big Red watched back, looking for the tell-tale sign. The lack of surprise. The give-a-way twitch.

"What's that mean?"

"It's a lesser sentence than first degree."

"How's that?"

"She had provocation. It appears he was choking her."

"That son-of-a-bitch choked her?" Color flushed his already ruddy face as anger raised his voice to a higher pitch.

"Appears that way. Now, tell me about the devil worshiping?"

"Why was he choking her?" He squirmed on the couch some more. His hands tightened into fists, and his lips thinned. "Son-of-a-bitch!"

"That was one of our questions." Big Red said. "Why do you think he would be choking her?"

Tobe let out a short, harsh breath of air. "He's always been one of them per-verts! That's why."

"How was he a pervert?"

"How the hell do ya think? He was into that strange kind of sex thing. He's a bully too. After the weak and helpless, you know, kids and women. Hain't got the balls to pick on a full-growed man, one that had a chance of fightin back." He clamped his teeth together a few time. "My Mary don't have no more strength than a kitten. She couldn't fight her way outta wet, paper sack."

"How do you know he's a bully and a pervert?"

"Talk spreads. Only know him to see him. Tell you the truth, somebody should of killed him years ago. Killin's all some men are fit for."

"Did Mary tell you about him?"

"Well, yeah, some I reckon. Didn't like him none a-tall. Didn't want nobody to know he was her pa. Don't know why she would be at his place to begin with. She feared him and that place worse than she feared a coiled rattlesnake. She hain't been back there since she left a long time ago."

"Did he sexually abuse Mary?"

"Now looky here, I know the law can use all kinds of stuff against a body. Besides, a man don't have to say nothing about his wife. It's the written law. Maybe she ought to have a lawyer or something? You know what you say can be used against you and that kind of stuff."

"I'm not trying to find out anything to harm Mary. I'm just after the truth."

"Truth is my wife needs some help. Them devil worshipers done tore her mind all to pieces. Reckon she can get it at that hospital you told me about. That's where she needs to be for a good while, anyhow. She takes spells, you know."

Big Red looked at him for a minute, knowing Tobias Tate was getting scared, wanting to stop talking, afraid he would give something away he shouldn't. Couldn't blame the man.

"The judge assigned her a free attorney. Where did she get the gun she shot him with? Was it yours?"

Tobe looked as though he was thinking about the gun. "Was it that pistol? Don't put no blame on me for that gun. She bought it a couple weeks back from a man up the road after she got spooked by them phone calls. He took advantage of her. Made her pay too much for it when she was scared."

"What phone calls?" Red looked up from his note pad.

"Them devil worshipers started calling her. Said she was going to burn before she died. Scared her near to death. She thought they were following her about. Got afraid to drive down the road by herself. I had to go with her when she took them dolls to sell."

"What dolls?"

"Them she made for the stores here about. Those hillbilly dolls the tourists buy."

"Is that how she earned money?"

"Yeah. She done it for over thirty years."

"Get much making dolls?"

"Naw. Buys groceries and gives her spending money's all."

"What do you work at?"

Tobias looked down at his feet and his head hung again.

"Laid off a couple weeks ago from the furniture factory down in Lenoir. Hope they'll put me back on soon. Hard to survive without working."

"Is that why Mary left you?"

His irritation at the question showed. "She didn't leave me over that. It was those crazy notions they put in her head. I only wanted her to get help. Like I said, her mind went at times. Made her do foolish things."

"By 'they' are you still referring to the devil worshipers?"

"Them and that crazy man-hater next door." Tobias moved his mouth like he was going to spit, instead he said, "That confounded old woman's got a cob stuck up her asshole and takes it out on all men. Told Mary for years, she ought to leave me."

Big Red wrote on his notepad. "Did you know her father had been committed to Broughton Hospital several years back?"

"So the talk went."

"He's been drawing disability since the day he was released. A man could get by on disability."

Tobe sat up straighter on the couch and gave Big Red an aggravated look. "Are you saying I want her committed so she can draw from the government?"

"No. I didn't say that at all. I wondered if you knew her father was on disability."

"I didn't know, or care about that man. Me and Mary both stayed away from him just like I told you."

"Mary didn't. Not today anyway." Big Red stood making sure his head didn't hit the light fixture hanging from the ceiling. "I may have to come back and ask you a few more questions." He went out the door without Tobias Tate getting up off the couch.

He saw the next-door neighbor standing not thirty feet away. Her white head bobbed up and down, as she appeared to be busy breaking dead flower heads off a geranium planted in the circle of a white painted, discarded tire.

"Good day to you ma'am."

She glanced toward Tobia's trailer, and then back at Big Red.

"You the sheriff?"

" Yes ma'am. I am."

Her voice lowered to a whisper as she stepped closer and leaned in. "You're here about her hain't you? Did they kill her? I knew they'd get her sooner or later."

"Who?"

"You know who I'm tag bout. Mary. Did the crazies kill her?"

"What crazies ma'am?"

"Those heathens that worship the devil. They've been stalking her. They telephoned her a dozen times a day. They drive by, too. I've seen their cars drive by here myself. They had her afraid out of her mind. Poor Mary. She never bothered nobody. Just minded her own business, she did. If that weren't bad enough on her, that man of her'n up and got fired. Laid off he claims, but I know better." She leaned within inches of his face and whispered. "He's trying to get rid of her you know. He wants to send her to Morganton. He claims she's crazy as a bed bug."

"How do you know this?"

"Why, they fight about it all the time. Sometimes it lasts way into the night. I can hear it plain as day. Them yelling at each other and so on."

"Did you know she was going to leave her husband?"

"She said she just wanted to get away for a few days. He wouldn't let her have no piece a mind. He took being fired out on her, he did. She tried to run him off a time or two, but he wouldn't go. Finally, she just up and left herself. Never said scat to me. Just walked out the door and down the road.

She didn't stop. Just kept right on walking till she was outta sight. I asked him," she jerked her head toward the trailer. "Where she went but he said for me to mind my own damned business. He cussed to me right like that, he did. Now, I'm not one to tolerate cussing, but he cussed a blue streak."

"I suppose Mary told you about the devil worshipers, didn't she?" Big Red asked.

"She did, and I heard the phone ringing off the hook time and again. Tore her up it did. Once, somebody broke in the trailer and tore pages on voodoo and stuff outta her encyclopedia and throwed it on her bed. Scared the fool outta her, it did."

"Did you see anyone break into her trailer?"

"It was done while I was at the grocery store. Mary took me there herself. We were both gone at the time it happened. She wasn't hardly in the house when I heard her hollering. I run over there to see what was wrong and the place was a mess. Papers on the bed. Books and clothes on the floor."

"Where was her husband?"

"Work I reckon. It was just before he got fired."

"What did Mary do?"

"It tore her nerves up something terrible. She was all for notifying you and having you do finger-printing and investigating stuff, but that man of her'n wouldn't allow it. Insisted it was just some kid pulling a prank."

"What do you think?"

"It's more'n that. A lot more."

The trailer door flew open and Tobias stepped out. The woman gave him an evil look. One which he returned.

"Well, is she alive or not?" The woman asked Big Red.

"She's alive," Big Red told her.

"Good. You better watch out for her. I gotta go afore he starts cussing me again."

She hurried into her trailer and closed the door. Tobias went back inside.

Chapter 4

Mary sat in the back seat of the patrol car and stared at the head of the driver. His momma let him lay too much as a baby. The back of his head was flat. Too bad he had short, cropped hair. Long hair would have hid it some. Made him look right quare, that flat head did.

The deputy sitting beside her, was reading from a paperback novel. There was the black outline of a contorted man with a gun on the cover. She didn't bother to look hard enough to see the title. She didn't like contorted men with guns. The deputy gave her sideways glances at regular intervals, as though she would disappear or turn into a raving monster if he didn't watch her. She put her hand on her stomach and looked at the deputy.

"Gall bladder problems," she said. "They want to operate."

The deputy looked at her as though she was a demon come to life.

She waited a minute before she spoke again. "My belly hurts."

"We'll be at the hospital in two hours. They can check you there."

She watched him readjust his position in the seat until he was leaning more against the car door.

It appeared he didn't like taking people to the Dorthea Dix hospital in Raleigh. He started reading again, and his body lost some tension as he turned a page.

"Wouldn't wake up."

Irritation at the interruption showed on his face. He frowned, narrowing his eyes. "What did you say?"

"They'd know I was asleep. I try never to sleep, but I doze off at times. They're gonna get me while I'm asleep. If they operate, I would never wake up."

"Who'll get you?"

"They speak in tongues, you know." She saw the driver glance in the rearview mirror at her, then back at the road. The car seemed to speed up. "You're a cop. You know all about them. They've got that place out near the Tennessee line where they gather at night. You've been there hain't you?"

"No ma'am." He let out a breath of air as he glanced down at his book like he wanted to get back to reading.

She nodded her head slow and easy. "It come to me one night. You know how things come to a body. Well, I was sittin in the dark. Didn't have any lights on. Knew they'd peek in the windows at me if I had lights on. They got this place out there on the mountain in the deep woods near the Tennessee line. You ought to go check that place out. There's skulls buried between tree roots. Two baby skulls, a lot of cat skulls." She frowned. "Don't know why they like cats, do you? Seems to me a dog ought to do just as well as a cat. Maybe some lambs. There's a lot of lambs sacrificed in the Bible, but they don't have a one out there. Must not know how to do things exactly right." She nodded her head. "I know why they sacrificed lambs. Have you ever smelled that meat cookin'? It stinks. A body might be able to eat it if it wasn't for the smell."

The deputy let his book rest on his leg and turned toward her. His pupils dilated slightly and his jaw muscles tightened. "Have you been to this place? What connections do you have with that bunch?"

She grinned. "I knew you'd heard of 'em. Want to take over things is what they wanna do."

"Have you been there?" he repeated.

"Just that one time, in my mind. Saw it plain as day, I did. Was the dead of night. They had a fire burnin' hot, sparks spittin' in the air higher than a man's head." Her hands gripped each other in her lap. She pressed her bony back into the seat and scrunched her body up as small as she could make it.

"Go on," the deputy encouraged.

"Listen! You're hearing it, hain't you? Those poor babies cryin'. Ought to be a law against hurtin' babies."

He frowned. "Do you know any of these people? The ones that hurt babies?"

Her hands loosened their grip on each other as her fingers picked at a sore spot on the back of her hand.

"No," she said at last. "Not them. Don't know 'em, but I was in the grocery store the other day when one of 'em walked up to me right close and whispered, 'Prepare thyself for deceasement.' He scared the livin' daylights outta me! I screamed for somebody to grab him. Folks turned and looked at me like I was out of my mind! The man walked away as pretty as you please." She shook her head. "Folks just don't listen do they?"

"Which grocery store?"

"That big un. You know, the Winn Dixie." She glanced up at the deputy and lowered her voice as though she was telling him a secret. "I think Birdie, my mother-in-law, is one of them devil worshipers."

The deputy grinned. "I've thought the same thing about my mother-in-law."

Her eyes grew wide in her thin face. "Watch your children!"

"What?"

"Watch your children. If your mother-in-law is one of em, she's liable to take your babies and have them sacrificed." She leaned closer him and whispered. "They don't kill all the children. For some of em, death would be better."

She closed her eyes and took a deep breath of air from inside the closed squad car. Her hand rubbed at her face.

When she opened her eyes she noticed he was looking at her hands, swollen red places, scratches and scrapes.

She moved her hands from her face. "I think I'd be all right if I could stop hearin' those babies cry. You ever have a ringin' in your ears that wouldn't stop? I have their cryin' in mine."

Part Two

Legacy of Abuse

1911
A family history

Chapter 5

Jay was born on Hemlock Ridge in 1911 to Pete and Alva Press. A hell of a place to be born, but folks that lived there didn't know it. It was home to them.

Folks saw the rocks that littered the land as something to be moved into piles. Rocks could be right handy. A snake could be killed with a rock. Rocks made a good fence if stacked right, or a house if a body was determined enough. The steep hillsides made the rocks easier to roll while bare feet gripped the ground.

It made a man have to learn to walk sideling as he turned the hill ground with the mule and plow. Strong muscles developed from holding straight the ever-sliding plow. Steep hills made men out of boys, and non-workdays made boys out of men.

The mule didn't much care how steep the ground was. A mule did what he had to do when he had to do it.

Most men cared. Pete Press didn't. He didn't care much for nothing. He wanted to be left alone. He liked to look at the far mountain range as it turned from blue to ebony as night came on. He liked to watch the buzzards circle in the air. Pete liked to hear the squirrels quarrel and see the birds gather to migrate. He liked to hear the sound of running water, and he like the feel of the wind on his naked skin. But he didn't like to sweat on a hot summer day. He didn't like to freeze on a cold winter day. He liked spring and he liked fall when the weather was just right.

What he liked most of all was pokin'. He just couldn't seem to get enough of it. Alva was right agreeable at first. She didn't like it much when she was as big as a yearling heifer before Jay was birthed. She hadn't liked it since. Jay was nine days old now. She had better start liking it again. He had to have him a poke. Craved it like a thirsty man craved a cool drink of water. He flat out believed he would die of deprivation if he didn't get a poke soon.

Through his mind, he ran all the female women he knew. There ought to be one of them willing to let him have a poke. The only one he knew for certain would be agreeable was old Bessie. She was snotty nosed and snaggled toothed and flat out older than the dirt he was standing on. Old Bessie charged a man a nickel or a paper sack full of store candy. More'n likely rotted her teeth sucking on candy. He didn't have a nickel and he didn't have candy. Alva had just better be willing.

Pete Press didn't finish his plowing, although he had two good hours of daylight left and could of finished before nightfall. He unhooked the plow right were it stuck in the ground. No need to tote it home then tote it back up the hill tomorrow. He stripped the mule of its harness and left him to find his own way to water and grass.

He found Alva milking the cow in the shelter he had nailed up next to the hog lot. That way one side could serve as a barn for the hog and the other side as a barn for the cow. He liked to think of it as a barn. If he were truthful, he'd have to admit it was just a pile of nailed together scrap lumber he had scavenged. But it was better than nothing, and it would do until he could do better. Lumber didn't come cheap.

He had traded old man Clark five years of promised work for five acres of land when he took Alva as his wife. For four months now, he had worked for Clark three days a week. A man had to work for himself the other four days. Clark agreed that was the right and just way of doing things.

Still, five years was a mighty long time when it was ahead of you.

A bunch of the neighbors helped him cut saplings and make a one-room cabin to live in. He had wanted good Poplar logs, but they weren't to be had on his five acres, and he couldn't afford to buy them. So, saplings it was. The cabin stood fine and kept most of the rain and wind out, but got mighty cold during the winter when snow blew through the cracks. Finally, Alva dabbed the cracks full of mud. Took her a while being the ground was frozen most all winter.

He saw Alva stand up from where she had been milking and go to the house. He hurried after her. He noticed Jay was asleep in the washing tub. Alva had crammed it full of empty feed sacks to make it softer for him to lie in.

"You can wait a minute to strain that," he told Alva.

"You ain't in that all fired hurry. What you wantin any how?" Alva asked as she strained her milk into a gallon jar.

Pete knew she wanted to take it to the creek and set it in the cold water, but he stood in her way.

"I need to poke."

"Humph!" she gave a disgusted snort. "Shoulda backed that mule up to a stump."

Pete didn't like her getting contrary with him. Even a fool knew mules kicked. Alva had a mouth on her that equaled any man. Alva herself equaled any man. He felt proud of that. A man didn't want a beanpole of a woman, broke under duress. A smart man wanted him a big woman that could outwork a team of mules and was soft when he poked her.

"You aim to lay down in the floor or do you want me to put you there?"

Alva gave him a look that made a few of his body hairs raise up. He knew she had it in her to be as mean as a grizzly bear. It was a good thing he married her when she was young enough to be handled.

He lifted his hand and gave her rounded hind end a stinging slap.

"Watch that heavy hand of your'n. Someday you might wake up without nothin to poke with."

Alva said it so quiet like it spooked him some, but he'd never let her know it. He had never let anybody know she troubled him for being the way she was.

Alva saw the mean look in his eyes and lay down in the floor and lifted her chop-sack dress above her belly to keep any stain from getting on the material.

Pete took one look at the bloody rag she had stuck between her legs. He didn't want a bloody poke. He rolled her onto her belly.

"What you doin?" she demanded.

"More'n one way to skin a mule. More'n one way to poke."

It took Pete all the next day to finish up two hours of plowing. Alva was beginning to wonder if he was going to have the garden ready to plant before it was harvest time. She'd say something to him, but she knew it would do no good. Pete went at his own pace in his own time.

Besides, she didn't like a quarrel, and there was no need to start one without a reason. Course Pete gave her reason morning, noon, and night, but she tried to ignore him although it was a tough thing to do.

She reminded herself that the preacher said women were born to have things rougher than a man. Preacher said it was because they eat that apple in the Garden of Eden. He said a man shouldn't be blamed cause the woman fed the apple to him. A woman was supposed to feed her man.

Well, she fed Pete and she let him poke her whenever he wanted to. She had things a lot rougher than Pete, but it didn't make her feel any more religious. On the contrary, she felt she had been cheated out of something. Kind of like the good things in life were held out for the men. Maybe the preacher was right. Maybe that was woman's punishment for the apple. Well, if that was so, she hoped that had been one fine eatin' apple.

Chapter 6

Remember thy Sabbath Day and keep it Holy. Pete Press took it literally in that Sundays were a time of rest, Alva noticed as she came in from milking the cow. He was still in bed. He had woke up long enough to move Jay from the bed to the washtub in the furtherest corner of the cabin. Jay was screaming to the top of his lungs and kicking his legs into the air. Alva let him scream while she strained her milk and screwed the lid on the jug.

"Shut that racket up!" Pete yelled.

Alva paid him no mind as she went to Jay. She took the baby from the tub and laid him on the floor where she changed his wet, soiled diaper. His screams were so powerful his face was tinged with blue by the time Alva put him to her breast. He latched on and sucked with hungry determination.

"You greedy thing," Alva said, but did not coo. She didn't believe in silly baby talk. Her son was going to grow into a strong man, not one expecting sweetsie, cutesie stuff. When he had emptied one breast, she laid him on his belly across her knees to burp. He wanted nothing to do with burping. He hungered for the other breast. Alva gave it to him and watched as contentment claimed her little man.

After her son had sucked his fill, Alva put the iron on the back of the cook stove to heat while she fixed breakfast. She should have ironed Pete's clothes yesterday, but didn't want to take a chance on getting a wrinkle in them overnight. Nobody was going to whisper how she didn't take proper care of Pete's clothes.

When breakfast was over, Alva dipped hot water out of the water closet connected to the stove into the washtub. Pete got in and sat down. She scrubbed him from head to toe with the washrag, paying special attention to his fine head of hair and dirty ears. Alva made sure she rinsed all the soap out real good.

"Damn you woman," Pete complained as rinse water got into his eyes. "Stupid careless bitch."

Alva sat the bucket of water down on the swept-dirt floor and walked away. She stepped out the door, carried in an arm-full of stove wood and fed it into the firebox of the cook stove. She moved the pot of pinto beans onto the hot part of the stove and poured more water into the pot. They should be done by the time church was over.

She knew Pete sat there, watching her, waiting for her to come back to him, dry him off, and hand him his pressed Sunday clothes.

"Damn it! What's takin you so all fired long? This water's gettin cold as a witch's teat."

"You cuss me, you dry your ownself off."

Alva saw by the look in Pete's eyes that he wanted to come back at her. Knew he wanted to slap her up the side of her head. He gave her an ill, warning look like she was about to push him too far, but Alva didn't care. She watched as Pete stood up, dripping into the water, got the chop sack towel, and dried himself off.

Alva didn't have time to wash herself good and proper in Pete's tub of water. She dropped her dress, stepped into the water, grabbed soap and washrag and began scrubbing the sweat from her body. Someday soon she was going to sit down in a tub of warm water and enjoy it, but it wouldn't be today.

It took thirty minutes to walk to the church house, a small white building constructed years in the past, but still good enough for preaching the Gospel to mountain folks.

Alva had a dislike for Hal Holloman, the preacher of Hemlock Ridge Baptist Church. How he got to Hemlock Ridge was a matter of speculation to her, even though Hal talked about his arrival often.

Alva took a seat near the back of the church on the left hand side. Men sat on the right hand side, as they were the right hand of God. She suspected it was God's left hand that got most of his work done.

Alva wanted easy access to the door if Jay cried. Nobody was going to say she let her baby interrupt the preaching.

Bobbie was her little sister by two years. She slipped onto the bench beside her. Bobbie shivered in her thin cotton dress as she rubbed her bony arms with her hands. Alva looked at her and kept from shaking her head right there in the church house. Bobbie was little more than a helpless mouse, always afraid of something. Too bad she didn't take more after her than she took after their mother.

"Maw can't come," Bobbie whispered. "Back's painin' her something awful."

"Her time?" Alva whispered back.

Bobbie nodded. "She sent word for you to come soon as preachin's over. I'm to take the boys to the river. Let 'em catch supper. Maw said it weren't fittin' for men and boys to be around."

"Pap?"

"Left out at daybreak totin' his rifle. Maw said for you not to come till after preachin', and say nary a word to a soul."

Alva could believe that. Maw was nigh onto being an embarrassment for she was too old to be fooling around having younguns. Eleven of anything was more than plenty. She ought to have enough gumption to tell Pap where he could put his poker. But Alva knew Maw never said scat to a fly. It'd have to suck her blood for a week before she'd smack it.

Alva looked over at the boys sitting on the bench next to Pete showing faces that weren't scrubbed as usual, and hair that wasn't combed neat with the precision part Maw knew how to make. There was mischief shining in their eyes when they looked at each other. Alva knew they were hatching some plan of meanness to get into after church was over. Poor little Bobbie was too much like Maw to control nine boys. Alva knew one swipe of her hand and she would put them in line, but she wouldn't have time. She'd have to hurry to Maw.

Preacher Holloman rose from his chair near the pulpit. "Sister Maime, would you kindly turn your hymn book to Amazing Grace and get God's children flowin' with song."

Maime, with rod-straight back, puckered lips and furrowed brow took the request with fervor and determination. Alva watched Preacher Holloman's eyes scan the congregation. Alva saw him look to Maw's regular place and knew he realized why Maw was missing. His black eyes came to rest on Bobbie and lingered. His tongue snaked out to moistened thick lips until they settled into a satisfied position.

His wife sat on the front row with her mouth moving but not actually singing outloud. Everybody knew her voice was a squawking irritation interrupting the singing, but it was her place to pretend to sing. Mrs. Holloman was as lean as a willow switch. Her hair was a dirty colored blonde and her skin was so white that blue veins stuck up from underneath. Every time Alva looked at her, she wanted to give her a good worming. Alva thought Mrs. Holloman, Ester to some, appeared to be the perfect preacher's wife, head hung with reverence and lacking enough spunk to sit straight on a church bench. Alva could tell by looking that she was too puny to get in a family way. A spindly slip of a corn stalk never produced a fit ear of corn. Woman must have something going wrong with her on the inside. Guess the preacher couldn't pray God into giving him a healthy wife. Alva suspected preacher Holloman needed to work on a more direct praying line between him and God. She also knew a different preacher for Hemlock Ridge Baptist Church would suit her mighty fine, but it wasn't up to her to advocate such a thought. Folks said God ordained preachers and it wasn't up to mortal humans to judge them.

When it was about time for preaching to end, Alva watched Preacher Holloman get his second wind. He cupped his left hand over his left ear and shouted. "Praise God Almighty! Whee-uh! Give unto man what is man's and give unto God what is God's." He rushed from the pulpit, down the aisle, to the back of he church in a half-run, half-strut. His right hand shot out and caught Bobbie by her thin shoulder. "Lord God on high, look down on this sinner and bring her into your fold."

Bobbie's pale face turned whiter than clabbered milk as she seemed to shrink in on herself.

"Child, Child! Give yourself unto God. Come to the front of the Church and bow down in humility to Him. Let yourself be saved from your sins!"

Bobbie was big-eyed with panic as she looked at Alva.

"Whee-uh!" The preacher shouted again causing baby Jay to wake up with a squeal like a scared pig. The preacher's hand yanked in an attempt to pull Bobbie into the aisle. He would have succeeded if Bobbie's arms hadn't grasped Alva around the stomach and desperately hung on.

The preacher pulled, Bobbie clung, and Jay screamed. Alva let her glaring eyes come to rest on the preacher's face. She leaned close enough him to smell Juicy Fruit chewing gum on his breath. Something came over her. It was as if she was possessed by a different being. The being said two words to her.

"Stop this!"

Alva moved until her lips touched the outer rim of Preacher Holloman's ear. She whispered low enough that the congregation couldn't hear. "Get away from her afore I crack your balls like a thin-shelled nut!"

His mouth opened as though he was going to let out another whee-uh, but this time he sucked air like he was trying to take up all the air in the church house. His hand came loose from Bobbie and raked through his greased hair. He rushed down the aisle, back to his pulpit and shouted.

"Lord God Almighty help this wicked child come to you. Let her see her evil ways and repent!"

A few shallow shouts rose from the A-men corner, but mostly quick glances peeked at Alva, then away. Her heavy breast was openly revealed as she let baby Jay suck his fill.

Chapter 7

"You take them boys to the river," Alva told Pete in the churchyard.

Alva made sure no one else heard her. She knew the congregation had nodded their hellos or good bys and eased away as fast as possible with their memory of her exposed breast, but she didn't much care what they saw when her boy needed feeding. She didn't stop to think what they might say as she usually did.

"I han't eat yet," Pete objected.

"Won't hurt you none. Maw's in a bad way." She turned her back on Pete and took a few steps, then stopped and looked back. Bobbie was following Pete. "Bobbie."

Bobbie's unwilling eyes looked at Alva. A slight motion of Alva's head brought Bobbie to her. They walked on together, toward Maw.

Alva heard the boards on the front porch moan as they moved under her feet. She pushed the door open and found Maw in bed. Maw had placed the oilcloth, she used at hog killing, on the bed to protect it from the birthing. Alva wondered why she used the good bed and not the floor. Birthing on the bed made a mess to clean up and Maw didn't like messes.

"You're on the bed?" Alva knew she had disapproval in her voice, but Maw ought to known better than to ruin good bedclothes.

A weak voice answered. "I aim to die in a soft bed."

Alva looked down and saw there was blood dripping on the floor. She shoved Jay into Bobbie's arms. "Put him in the kitchen then get back here."

She flipped the hand-stitched sheet, the one with a hog's face printed on it, from on top of Maw. The oilcloth couldn't hold all the blood mixed with broken birth water. The fluid had soaked the quilts, the feather tick, and gone into the stuffed mattress. Alva bent down and looked under the bed. A puddle had formed with a continuous drip adding to it.

"Hell!" She took a couple of deep breaths. "Why didn't you send for me sooner?" She yanked Maw's petticoat up past her shriveled breasts. No milk. A sure sign there were bad problems. Maw was nothing but a bag of bones with precious little flesh.

"She not eat?"

"Couldn't," Bobbie said. "Puked a lot."

Alva knew Maw never ate much when she wasn't brooding. No wonder she didn't have strength enough to push a baby out.

"Bring me Pap's liquor. All you can find. Maw can you bear down any?" Her voice was insistent. "Can you?"

Maw's eyes looked up at Alva and she smiled weakly. "Done that," she whispered. "Don't hurt much no more. Don't want to push."

Alva placed her hand on Maw's stomach. She could feel the baby inside as plain as feeling through thin cloth. Maw wouldn't be pushing it out. The womb had gone limp. It was pull the baby out and hope one of them might live or let them both die.

Alva thought about her two choices.

Somehow, it came to her she ought to prefer the second on Maw's account, but she knew she would do the first. A body couldn't let her own Maw die.

"Get to the barn loft," she told Bobbie as Bobbie set two jugs of corn liquor on the floor by Alva's feet. "Get into the fodder and find a lot of smut or Maw's dead for certain."

"I hain't afeard of dyin'," Maw's voice was faint. "Hit's a sight easier than livin'."

Alva paid no mind to Maw's words as she poured liquor over Maw's body from her stomach down. It didn't matter if it soaked the bed more. Things had to be cleaned anyway and white liquor was the best disinfectant there was. She splashed liquor over her own hands to above her elbows. She knew what had to be done, and nobody was ever going to say she didn't do it.

She didn't flinch as her hand eased deep into Maw. It had to be done.

Maw's mouth opened wide, but only a thin whimper came out as her eyes rolled back in her head. She was silent with her mouth still gaping open. Alva hoped she was dead, knowing it would be for the best. Maw had been through enough hell in her short years. A husband of the worse kind, too many crying, hungry children, and no hope of anything ever being any better. It just wasn't right for Maw to be going through this, but a shallow breath lifted her scrawny chest.

Alva felt the baby and knew it was in the right position for birth. It felt little. A number twelve baby that size should have slid out like a greased spoon.

Alva knew, just as sure as she was standing there, that Maw didn't want the baby out. Maw wanted to die. She wanted to leave behind hard work and grubbing for food to feed ten kids, a husband, a farm full of animals and herself. She didn't want her back aching while she scrubbed clothes on a washboard in a tub she'd hauled water from the creek to fill.

She didn't want to drag her body out of bed at five o'clock in the morning, after being kept up all night with a colicky baby, then have to work all day and into the night just to feed them all enough to stay alive.

She just wanted rest and the only way to get any rest was through death. Alva knew. She knew the way Maw was, but it made no difference to what had to be done. What she had to do.

Alva's calloused hand gripped the slimy head of the baby and her stubby fingernails dug into its skull. She pulled with all her strength. Maw's body arched, giving one last attempt to rid itself of the burden it harbored.

The baby came out just as Alva expected. It wasn't much bigger than a newborn pig and was as blue in color as the blossom on blue-eyed grass. Her first instinct was to throw it onto the floor, but she didn't. She raked mucus from its little face, then held it up by its little feet while pulling the lumpy cord out of Maw.

Alva hated this thing on sight. This little, bitsy, girl child. It was nothing but trouble that never should have been. She placed it on the oilcloth as she ripped strips from Maw's petticoat and tied the cord off twice. She went into the kitchen, came back with the butcher knife and made the cut.

She grabbed the corn stalks, their husks deformed with pouches of smut, from Bobbie and began packing Maw to stop her hemorrhaging. When done, she put her hand on Maw's stomach and massaged the womb with near vicious strength, knowing the lax womb could allow her maw to bleed to death if she didn't make it contract.

Bobbie carefully reached past Alva and picked up the tiny baby from the oilcloth, and disappeared into the kitchen.

Minutes later, Alva heard a mewing sound like a weak kitten might make.

"Well, shit," Alva said as she watched the hemorrhaging slow down until clots of blood came from Maw's body. Looked like both of them had a chance at living.

Chapter 8

Alva worked Maw's womb like a piece of bread dough until she thought her arm would drop off. Everytime she stopped it would go limp and she would have to rub fast and hard to make it contract enough not to hemorrhage. A dozen times, she wondered why she was going to all this trouble to make Maw live. Maw wanted to die so why didn't she just let her? At thirty-one years of age Maw would live another year, until Pap knocked her up again. Then she would die for certain. This womb wouldn't carry another baby to term. It would give way and there'd be nothing Alva could do the next time. Alva knew this as certain as she knew daylight would come with morning. She knew it would be easier on Maw if she died now. Pap would just go find him a young girl to marry up with. There were plenty of young girls out there who would marry the first man that asked them.

There weren't enough men to go around. Besides, what else was there for a woman? Work yourself to death for your own husband and kids, or end up working yourself to death for somebody else's? She chose working for Pete and her ownself. There had been several girls eyeing Pete until she set them straight by letting them know she was marrying Pete Press. If she hadn't, she would be responsible instead of Bobbie.

It'd be easier on Bobbie if Pap got him a young wife. The way things stood now, Bobbie would have to take Maw's place doing all the work and caring for the new baby, if it lived. A young wife could do her share of the work.

Finally, when daylight was growing dim, Maw's eyes began to roll in their sockets. Her eyelids fluttered up and down like they didn't know if they wanted to open or stay closed. After some time, they opened a crack then a crack more.

"So, you're awake," Alva said.

Maw didn't speak, but her eyes opened all the way.

"You bled worse than a stuck hog. I wouldn't a give a plug nickel to a greenback you'd ever come back to life again. Dead to the world you was."

Maw looked at Alva and her eyes got bigger and bigger.

Alva watched Bobbie tiptoe into the room with the baby wrapped in a towel she'd warmed in the cook-stove oven. Bobbie went to Maw's side and held the baby near her face.

"Look at your baby girl, Maw. She's alive and I'm carin' for her real good."

Maw didn't look or speak. Her face settled into a blank, non-expression and her eyes took on a distant look. One single tear oozed from her right eye, slid down her cheek, and dripped into the thin twist of graying hair lying on her neck.

"Take her back into the kitchen, Bobbie. Maw han't herself yet."

Bobbie left and Maw closed her eyes. Alva rubbed and silently quarreled at herself for not having enough guts to let them both die. This world wasn't no place for the weak and tender hearted. She told herself she had no business being either one. It just didn't pay.

A while later, mewing cries came from the baby and Bobbie brought her back to the bed.

"She's starvin'," Bobbie said proudly. "Look at that little mouth goin' for her fist."

Alva squeezed Maw's teat and shook her head. There wasn't one drop of the yellow life-giving milk, not even a speck of clear liquid. Alva took the baby from Bobbie's arms with a frown between her brows.

"You rub this here knot. You rub it hard as you can. If you slack up, she'll bleed again. Don't want her to die now that I've nearly kilt myself keepin' her alive."

Bobbie began to rub as Alva pulled her large breast from her dress bodice and let her nipple fill the small mouth. The sucking was slow and weak. Nothing at all like her boy's. She made herself a vow right then and there. Never in her life would she give birth to something as frail and puny as this. She'd have big healthy babies or she'd have none at all.

"Maw?" Bobbie said. "Maw, you awake?"

She didn't answer, nor did she move.

"Maw?"

"She's restin'. Don't go botherin' her none right now. What you want anyway?"

"She ought to have a name. Being she's number twelve, I wondered if I could name her Lacy?"

"Seems you could. Don't reckon it's gonna bother Maw none one way or another. Nor nobody else, for that matter."

"Maw's gonna live ain't she?" There was a faint quaver to Bobbie's voice.

Alva looked at Bobbie, saw her face, slim and open, a face just like Maw's. Her brown eyes were a little frightened permanently as though life scared her. A thirteen-year-old girl such as Bobbie wasn't in fit shape to take on nine boys, Pap and a sickly baby. She didn't have the guts for all that work. Bobbie needed to learn to be more like her if she was going to survive in this world.

"She is gonna live?" Bobbie repeated

"She will if she wants to," Alva said as she watched Bobbie look at Maw's pale face while she rubbed the loose, excess skin on Maw's shrunken belly.

Bobbie wouldn't let her eyes linger on the two hanks of shriveled flesh hanging near the insides of Maw's armpits that were her breasts. Instead, she looked at the graying hair, thin and clumped into wet strands that had wallowed free from a bun at the nape of her neck.

Poor little Bobbie, Alva thought, and wondered how she got to be made of such flimsy stuff. Took after Maw, she reckoned. She sure didn't take after her. Alva took pride in her own strength and determination.

"Why wouldn't she want to live?" Bobbie asked, wide eyed with concern.

"Can't say," Alva answered. "I just can't say."

Near dark, Pete brought the boys home carrying a heavy string of catfish, blue gills, and hammerhead carp.

"Clean 'em," Alva told Pete when he came into the room. "I'll cook 'em along with some taters and beans for supper. Looks like I'm havin' to spend the night. Maw ain't doing no good. You can milk back at home and feed the hog yourself."

Pete walked out the door. "You Clayton. Alva said for you to clean that mess of fish."

Alva knew Clayton heard what she said, but Clayton wasn't going to put up a fuss with his maw laid out near death's door. Clayton was a lot like Bobbie. Instead, he turned to the next two oldest boys. "Dean, Evert, you two best get the cow milked if you be wantin' milk with our supper."

Alva watched as Frank, followed by Grady, went off to the hen house to search for eggs. The others wandered off to play somewhere while baby Kyle sat on the ground alone, crying until his nose dripped into the dirt of the yard.

Eventually, Alva saw Bobbie, carrying Lacy, come out and take him into the kitchen where she built up the fire to cook supper.

Alva didn't see Pete and knew he was long gone. He had his own cold milk in the creek branch, and it wouldn't take anything to heat up his pot of beans. Alva knew they would be cooked done by now.

Bobbie felt a deep sadness as she watched Maw closely. Maw lay there in bed letting Bobbie spoon soup and soft food in her mouth. Sometimes she would swallow on her own, sometimes not. Never had she looked at anyone, never had she said a word.

"Swallow it, Maw," Bobbie said. "I fixed this broth just for you."

Maw swallowed, but the look in her eyes appeared to be far away, as though she was lost in another world.

The birds were singing outside the front room window where her bed was. The boys were playing, fighting, or crying, but Maw didn't hear that. It was the birds, the sweet, sweet sound of the birds, that filled Maw's mind and took her back in memory to a place that was good.

She wasn't big, just a little squirt lying beneath the Rusty Coat Apple tree. There was a world of white blossoms touched with pink above her. She laughed as the wind stirred and petals filled the air and floated downward, touching her face, her body, her mind. A pair of birds were singing to each other in the branches, darting and flirting with each other as their song filled the air. She watched them and smiled and smiled.

Bobbie thought Maw was smiling because Lacy was on the bed next to her.

"Hain't she cute, Maw?" Bobbie cooed. "Hain't she the cutest little thing you ever did see?" Bobbie asked, wondering why Maw just sat and stared far off like she was doing. Why wasn't she talking, saying something.

Maw's face showed pleasure as she sniffed the sweetness of apple blossoms and the spice of the earth she lay on. The world was good when spring came and the sun warmed the skin. There was no cold wind to blow, nor snow to make tender skin ache. Living was easy when winter was no longer there to hurt you.

Bobbie finished feeding Maw and changed the pad underneath her hips before she picked up Lacy in one arm and carried her, along with the bowl of broth, into the kitchen. She sat the bowl and spoon in the dishpan to be washed later. She hollered out the back door. "Clayton. Where are you at?"

He came through the door with an armload of stove wood. "What you hollerin' at me for?"

"I've got to run over the hill with Lacy. Alva's got to let her suck. You'll have to look after Maw and the boys while I'm gone."

Clayton's eyes, as blue as Pap's, looked at Bobbie as though there were a hundred questions he wanted to ask her and was afraid of what the answers might be. "Why don't Alva keep her being she's the only one can feed her?"

Bobbie smiled at the boy who had grown way too big for his clothes, but not big enough to do the work of a man. She couldn't help wishing he would grow faster, become a man sooner than was possible. There was a lot that needed doing, a lot she feared she couldn't do. "She's got a pile of work that keeps her busy. She's got baby Jay to tend to."

"Hain't no more'n you do. Kyle and Jarred are babies and you have to tend to them and Maw."

"I'll hurry," she said.

The buds on the trees were swelling, Bobbie noticed, as she cut through the woods and headed for he creek. She wished she could slow her pace a bit in order to look close at the Sarvice trees, maybe break off a few twigs and bring them home to put into a canning jar full of water. They were fixing to bloom out their showy white, but she didn't have time to want pretty things right now.

Lacy was hungry. She had fixed a sugar-tit, a rag with a hunk of brown sugar twisted into a little knot the size of Lacy's mouth. Lacy sucked at it and whimpered. At home, Bobbie dribbled drops of cow's milk in her mouth with a spoon to stretch out her feeding time with Alva, but it didn't satisfy her. Bobbie climbed through the barbwire fence on the ridge and hurried down the hill. She saw Pete on the far hill sitting in the shade cast from the huge trunk of an Oak tree. She lifted her hand and waved.

She found Alva dragging deadfall to the chopping block to cut up for stove wood. Alva dropped the limb, and then turned toward Bobbie. "Maw ain't got no milk yet?"

"Don't reckon she's gonna have none."

"Humph." Alva snorted in her normal disapproving way. "You have been checkin' to see? You hain't too squeamish to do that are you? Least Maw could do is give a little milk."

"She can't help it none," Bobbie said softly as she looked at the fuzz of hair on Lacy's head. "Maw ain't doin good a tall. "

"You runnin' cross that hill five times a day hain't any good either."

"It hain't nothing. I rather be out in the woods than shut up inside the house." But Bobbie didn't want to be running to Alva. Everything was a bother to Alva. A bother she acted like she shouldn't have and didn't want. "Where's Jay?"

"In the house where this wind can't hit him. You better keep this scrawny thing covered up good as you tote her all over creation. If she gets a cold, she's a goner for certain."

Bobbie noticed that Alva didn't have Lacy covered up very good as she let her suck. She wondered why Alva didn't seem overly fond of the helpless little thing. "You don't like Lacy much, do you?"

Alva puckered her brows. "I like her fine."

"What is it then?" Bobbie persisted. "I'd like to know."

Alva frowned down at the little thing tugging gently on her breast. "Maw was plumb used up during the spell she was carryin' this youngun, and Maw knew it. Wouldn't even push her out into the world. I'm thinkin' there ain't no way on God's green earth this baby is gonna to be right. If she does live, she'll remain dried up and worthless. She'll never make no kind a woman. You can mark my word on that."

Bobbie looked at the perfect round face and the tiny hands. Why, Lacy was a little doll of a baby. She was just a small baby girl, nothing like Jay or the boy babies Maw had. There was nothing wrong with this sweet little baby. She'd show Alva that Lacy would grow up to be a fine woman. She'd make sure of it if she had to bring her to Alva ten times a day.

"Are you poorly on givin' milk?" Bobbie asked. "I wouldn't want to rob Jay if you don't give enough."

"No, I ain't," Alva sounded irritated, and looked it.

Bobbie managed not to grin.

Alva gave Bobbie a bewildered look. It was almost an insult for Bobbie to even think she couldn't produce more than enough of anything. She had never seen the day she was not in fine health, and she intended to stay that way.

Chapter 9

Ester Holloman was sitting on the warped, weathered planks of the porch steps when Bobbie got back home. It was the first time Bobbie had seen Ester other than at the church house. It was a known fact Ester never got out and visited the neighbors like a preacher's wife was supposed to do. Folks didn't think hard about her though. They could tell she was the sickly type and wasn't fit for doing much work.

"You feelin' poorly?" Bobbie asked.

Ester was slumped sideways and breathing hard. The blue veins stood out in her face like crooked pieces of colored string. Her temples were indented deep and her pulse throbbed visibly beneath the pale, thin skin. Sweat covered Ester's upper lip and dampened the armpits of her dress as though she had been doing hard labor.

She shook her head. "Evenin', Bobbie. I'm feeling right good today. Good enough to pay you a visit." She tried to smile. Her lips stretched. "Clayton said for me to wait out here on you."

"Don't you want to come inside and sit a spell?"

Ester shook her head again. "The breeze feels good. I was a little warm after that long walk. You live farther back than I thought, and it was through the woods."

Bobbie sat down beside her. Ester looked at the sleeping baby with a longing in her eyes that made Bobbie feel sad. It was like a woman starving for somebody else's bite of food. She thought about asking Ester if she wanted to hold Lacy, but didn't. Ester wasn't looking like she had the strength to hold a house fly, much less a wiggling baby.

"I brought you something," Ester said and pulled a baby bottle from her sweater pocket. "Heard your Maw can't feed her," Ester tried to smile and failed. "Your Maw has a baby and nothing to feed her, and I got a bottle and…" she hushed.

"Maw's not well." She longed to grab the bottle from the outstretched hand and kiss Ester Holloman at the same time. Lacy could eat now when she was hungry. She wouldn't have to depend on Alva to keep Lacy alive. "Where'd you get that?" she blurted out. Baby bottles weren't something folks kept on hand. There wasn't anything much helpful kept on Hemlock Ridge.

Ester held the bottle toward Bobbie. Her eyes looking at it as though she was giving away the very last bit of everything she had ever loved.

Bobbie took it, tucked it in the towel covering Lacy. "Thank God," she whispered.

A far away look came into Ester's eyes. A look that resembled Maw's. "I had a baby once, for a little while," Ester said.

Bobbie saw purple spider veins covering her entire eyelids when Ester squeezed her eyes closed. Moisture formed and gathered in her lashes, but Ester Holloman didn't cry.

"Nobody here knows about my little girl." Ester confesses. "She lived for five days with a hole in her heart. She was what they called a blue baby. Her skin had a tinge of blue and her little lips were dark blue, almost purple. She didn't have the strength to suck hard. Her breath would give out on her." She closed her eyes and dampened her lips with her tongue, then continued. "Hal said it was best if I didn't tell people about her. He said I'd forget faster that way. He said talking about things only kept it fresh in your mind. But he doesn't know what it's like to carry life in you, give birth to your baby, and then have it die. It leaves you hollowed out like there's nothing left inside. Emptiness, a frozen world of emptiness."

Bobbie longed to reach out and touch her, pat her shoulder or maybe the top of her head. Say words that would ease the pained look on her face, but she didn't know what words to use when someone looked as pained as Ester.

Finally, Ester opened her eyes and stared off beyond the swept yard, toward the woods. Her face was blank of emotions, her eyes void of life.

"I told Hal he ought to give your Maw a few more days before he comes over here to pray. A woman that's given birth needs time to recover. You don't get over it in three days time. Nobody does."

Bobbie wanted to say something so she said, "Thanks for the bottle."

"I didn't have milk either." Ester went on as though Bobbie hadn't said a word. "That's why I got the bottle. It wouldn't have mattered if I had gallons of milk. My baby girl would have died anyway. You know, God don't let things live because they're loved. He don't make them die when they're not. Don't seem fair does it? There was nothing on earth or in heaven I loved more than my baby. Hal said that was why God took her. He said God was testing my faith by taking my precious baby. Hal said I loved her too much. He said God is a jealous God. Nobody is supposed to love nothing more than him."

She reached her hand out and let her slender finger touch the fuzz on the baby's head through a fold in the towel. Her chin trembled.

Bobbie watched her. "Do you need a dipper full of water or something?"

Ester withdrew her finger and rubbed the sweat specks from her upper lip with the back of her hand then pushed her thin hair from her forehead. Her other hand rested on her stomach, giving it just a little pressure.

"It's mighty hot for this early in the spring. I might could use some water. Would you mind carrying me a dipper full out here?"

Bobbie took Lacy inside and laid her down on the bed next to Maw's sleeping body. She got water from the bucket on the kitchen table and carried it to the porch.

Ester Holloman was gone. Bobbie poured the water on a scrawny weed trying to grow at the corner of the porch.

Two days later talk spread over Hemlock Ridge like dust on a hot, dry, windy day. Ester Holloman had died during the night while lying in bed beside her sleeping husband. Nobody knew exactly what had killed Ester, but everybody knew something had been wrong with her for a long time.

Bobbie thought she knew what that something was. She made Clayton stay home with the boys and Maw while she took Lacy with her to the funeral. She carried with her the precious bottle filled with cow's milk mixed with a spoon full of honey.

"I knew there was somethin' bad wrong with her," Alva whispered to Bobbie as they walked up the hill to the graveyard behind most everybody living on or around Hemlock Ridge. All the folks came out for the funeral. It wasn't often a preacher's wife died. "You ask me, she's lucky. I'd rather be dead than married to Preacher Holloman."

Bobbie looked at her sister with surprise. She never expected to hear such harsh words coming from Alva, especially about a preacher.

"He seems good enough."

"Good enough for what? Puttin' an apple in his mouth and roasting him like the greasy pig he resembles?"

Bobbie looked at her sister long and hard. "What's wrong?"

"Men! Hain't worth the snot they blow outta their nose." Alva moved Jay in her arm and tightened her lips.

Bobbie squirmed and looked off up the hill at the red clay dirt mounded up from the dug grave. Something was bothering Alva bad. She wondered what Pete had done, but she wasn't about to ask. Maybe it would be best to get Alva's mind elsewhere.

"Pap ain't come home yet. Clayton says he's layin' somewhere drunk. I don't see how a man can stay drunk for a week. Where's he gettin' liquor and food?" Bobbie looked down at Lacy, not nearly half the size of Jay.

"He's apt to be layin' out in some barn loft suckin' eggs and stealin' liquor. He'll come on back when he wants too."

"After this funeral is over, could you come by the house and look in on Maw? I've got her settin' up in bed and eatin' right good, but she han't said a word. She won't even look at Lacy. She acts quare in the head, real quare."

Chapter 10

Bobbie watched Alva lift Maw to a sitting position on the edge of the bed. "Put her shoes on," she told Bobbie.

Bobbie put faded socks then worn men's shoes without strings, on Maw.

"Maw, you're gonna get up off that bed and walk to the porch," Alva said firmly. "This hain't the first youngun you've had, and unless God has mercy on you, it hain't gonna be your last."

Maw seemed not to hear Alva's words. She sat there staring into space with a slight smile flicking her lips.

Maw heard her own pa talking in his gentle voice. "You ain't the first youngun to get a belly ache from eatin a bait of cherries," Pa told her as he placed a gentle hand on her head. "You won't be the last. What you need to do is get outta bed

*and set on the porch a while. You'll be fit as a
fiddle by the time night fall comes."*

*Oh how she loved the sound of her pa's voice.
There was so much love in it, such kind caring
words. Pa always had a minute of time for his
little girl. He was never impatient and mean. He
never whipped her. Pa lifted her up from the bed
and gave her firm support as he helped her onto
the front porch. She sat in the chair and thought
how right Pa was. The sun was warm and the birds
sang so pretty. It made her fell better just to know
pa was near her.*

"What do you think is wrong with her?" Bobbie
whispered to Alva as she watched Maw rocking in
the chair, a smile on her lips.

"Nothin'," Alva said firmly. "There's narry a
thing wrong except she wants some pettin'. This is
her way of getting out of work."

Bobbie frowned. She had never seen a time
Maw wanted petting. Maw always worked without
complaint from early morning until late into the
night. She never said much and she certainly didn't
complain. She just worked and did the things that
had to be done.

"She figures it's her time to get looked after, but
I certainly hain't got time to do it. I got my own
place now. I got Jay and Pete to take care of. As for

you, well she just up and left you to do everything around here. She had you to help her but you ain't got nobody."

"She's got me." Twelve-year-old Clayton said as he came around the corner of the porch, giving Alva a quarreling look like he wanted to argue.

Alva shook her head and gave a blowing sniff through her lips and nose. "You're still wet behind the ears. You hain't help like a man ought to be, nor a woman either."

"We'll make do till I get to be a man," Clayton said as he turned his back on Alva and headed for the barn.

"She's got me." Maw heard those words and frowned. Alvin Dyke said those words about her when she wasn't nothing but a pigtailed girl trying to catch fish from the river with her hickory pole and handmade hook.

Alvin Dyke had sandy blonde hair and the bluest eyes she'd ever seen. Lordy, was that boy good looking. All the girls at the meeting house were after him. She had him though. Yeah, she did. He was hers even if nobody else knew it. He only courted her, walked beside her when he took her home from church and sneaked a little sugar from her lips when nobody was looking.

He was hers all right. She snuck off and married Alvin Dyke.

Alvin talked her into running across the far hill with him, and it was done before she even thought about how her life would change. When her pa found out, tears filled his eyes. "I fear you'll live to regret hit," Pa had told her. "Time only will tell the truth, but I fear he's one of them no-accounts. Not a real mountain man a tall.

But she didn't want to think about Alvin. It made her head hurt. It made her heart hurt to think about her pa on his deathbed knowing for certain Alvin Dyke was one of the bad kind. She regretted marrying Alvin Dyke. She wasn't going to think on that either.

Bobbie saw Pap coming home carrying his gun in his left hand. Maw was still sitting on the porch rocking in the twine-bottomed chair, but Alva had gone home.

Pap looked at Maw then turned his head to see what she was seeing in the distance. There was nothing there but the woods.

"Stop your gawkin'," he demanded. "Git offa your lazy ass and git me food. I'm a starved man."

The speed of Maw's rocking increased but not so as would be noticed.

Her pa was on his bed saying: "Dyin's a good thing. It hain't to be fear'd. Peace. Glorious peace is to be had in heaven. Especially for those that have suffered here on earth."

Pap's foot hesitated on the top step before it came down loud on the porch plank. "You hear me old woman?"

Bobbie knew he couldn't figure what Maw was looking at. He lifted his right hand like he was going to strike her, but his hand hung there like a useless thing. The hand finally raked at his own sweaty head of hair.

"Pap," Bobbie's voice was a whispering sound, as though Maw couldn't hear a whisper. "Maw's not herself. Her mind's done left her."

"What tha hell, you say?"

"She hain't come around yet. Reckon all that pain and hurtin' took her mind from her for a spell. She'll be herself in a few days. I know she will."

A look of fear touched Pap's face, then disbelief, and then anger. "Hain't nary a thing wrong with her 'cept confounded laziness." He reached out and gave her shoulder a hard shove. Maw cackled with laughter as the rocker rocked harder. *"Ain't that swing fun?" Her pa said to her as he gave her*

*a push. "You enjoy it fur a spell, but I'll be needin'
the rope back tomorrow to haul in fire wood."*

*She laughed and laughed as the wind lifted her
skyward while she soared over the ground in her
rope-swing. The wind blew through her hair and
on her face. Life was good when you were a little
girl with a swing. Pap backed up a step and turned
to Bobbie.*

"You, gal, you fetch me some food. I'm near
starvation."

Bobbie went to the kitchen as she listened
to Pap searching for his liquor jugs. She hoped
he didn't remember how much liquor he'd left
behind. There wasn't enough, even though she
had watered it down some. Alva had used a lot on
Maw.

Pap hadn't even asked about the baby.

Bobbie knew Clayton had heard Pap's voice
and grabbed Lacy off Maw's bed in the front room
along with a feather pillow. She saw that Clayton
had hid her in the kitchen behind the warm cook-
stove, placing her in the middle of the feather
pillow.

Pap would drink liquor, eat food until his belly
pooched, then drink more liquor until he fell
asleep on the bed. Little Lacy would get mashed or
kicked out on the floor. Bobbie glanced at Clayton

as he sat near Lacy. His teeth were clinched tight, his eyes narrowed as he sat there listening to the boys playing out back of the house.

Bobbie sighed. Things had been peaceful while Pap was gone.

Bobbie watched Pap eat his food like a hungry dog. He hardly took time to chew. He guzzled milk as if it was spring water with no end to the supply. She, Maw and Clayton always drank milk sparingly because the small kids needed it worse. He wiped his mouth on the sleeve of his dirty shirt and looked up at her.

"You hain't the cook the old woman is."

"I know," Bobbie agreed. She didn't bother telling him he'd been eating her cooking instead of Maw's for a mighty long time.

"By supper time I expect you to have me some poke sallet fixed. I seed a bunch growin' all along the fence rows."

"I can do it, Pap." She put the last bit of cornbread and beans on his plate. She had been meaning to fix poke sallet but she had clean forgot about it while worrying over Maw and Lacy. She had Clayton pick a mess of creasy greens yesterday cause Maw loved them so. He had come back with mostly jackscrew, but she hadn't said nothing. Creasy greens and jackscrew was hard to tell apart. Jackscrew was mighty bitter to the taste and had a broader, healthier looking leaf which was to be expected. What wasn't fit for nothing always seemed to thrive better than the good stuff.

"You know better'n to let that poke get too big. It gets pizen in hit. Allus have to fry hit in lots of hog lard. Lard counteracts the pizen."

She wanted to tell him she knew that. Maw had her picking pokeberry sprouts when she was hardly big enough to walk, but she could never tell Pap anything. He'd say she was sassin' him and smack her in the mouth.

"Yeah, Pap. I'll watch."

"I got me a hankerin' for cobbler too. You sorry younguns hain't eat all them blackberries have you?"

"Maw still has a can or two put back. I'll get right to cookin' you one."

Pap nodded, stretched and got up from the table. A good meal deserved a good nap according to Pap.

Once Pap's snores were coming from the bed, Clayton crawled out from behind the stove.

"He drank all the milk. Lacy don't have none."

"It's all right," Bobbie told him gently. "You can milk a little early this evening. Besides, if worse comes to worse, you can run her over the hill to Alva."

"It'd make Alva mad."

"Her bein' mad don't matter if a baby needs milk. I do wish Maw would come to herself and start givin' milk. Lacy's such a pitiful little thing. She needs Maw. I do all I can, Clayton, but she needs Maw."

"She's got you," he hesitated then added, "and me. We're enough."

Bobbie saw anger along with determination flicker over his face. She frowned and looked at the top of the wood stove for a long time before she said, "Clayton why don't you go ahead and take Lacy to Alva. You can take a sack and pick poke sprouts on the way back."

Clayton looked behind the stove at the sleeping baby. "I'll take the boys and pick poke, but I han't takin' her there unless'un I have to."

Chapter 11

Alva had rigged a sling, hung it around her neck, and tied it around her waist, to carry Jay in as she went about her work in the garden. The garden was too far from the house to hear him when he cried.

She had planted onions, cabbage, lettuce, and peas the week before. Cold weather didn't hurt them none. Today she was planting a row of corn and beans. It was early in the season. They might get frost bit and killed, but she was willing to take a chance. She was craving fresh vegetables something fierce. She reckoned it was because she was having to make a pile of milk for Jay to suck, not to mention the odd times Bobbie showed up with Lacy.

Bobbie kept saying Lacy needed a little human milk ever day or so, but she knew what the real reason was. Pap was back home and there wasn't enough milk to go around. Pap always got his fill before the others had their turn. Maw's turn always came dead last.

Alva thought that was foolish. Back when she was at home and Maw made her do the cooking, she ate her fill outta the pot before the others had a bite.

Scrawny Bobbie hadn't learned that yet. She didn't have no more meat on her than a finger bone. Well, she had better learn fast or she'd be like Maw, too feeble to be in her right mind. Alva knew Maw didn't want to be in her right mind. Maw liked it right where she was.

Maw had let Pap beat all the want-to outta her years ago. She'd heard Maw beg and whimper while Pap slapped her. Maw would swear she'd never do it again if Pap would stop, but Pap never stopped, and Alva never knew what Maw promised not to do again. She figured the beatings were just because Maw was alive, and Pap was drunk and meaner than the Devil.

Alva would lay in the loft and wish the sounds would stop so she could sleep. Those sounds made her decided right off, the first man that laid a hurtful hand on her, she'd take his little finger off with the butcher knife while he slept. The second time, if it ever came, she would take the whole hand off with an axe.

It wouldn't ruin him for life. A one handed man could still work. Heavy work was about all a man was fit for, that and making babies.

So far, Pete only threatened her a time or two, but he was too much of a coward to ever carry out one of his threats. She never gave him credit for being smart, only credit for being scared of her.

"Mrs. Press."

Alva heard a strange voice and turned her head slow as her eyes locked in on him. The tenseness in her body relaxed as she recognized old man Clark.

"Yeah?" she questioned, as she looked him over real good. Why did folks insist on calling him old man Clark? He wasn't really that old. He was tall and straight backed with brown hair and eyes. His face was weathered dark. His hands were big as pie plates and appeared to be rough as a cob. They hung limply by his side. Idle power, she thought for she could see their strength. She couldn't help wishing Pete had hands like that, but it would take more than big hands to make a man out of Pete Dyke.

"Pete about?" Clark asked.

Alva frowned. Pete had left at daybreak to go to his place to work like he all ways does. "Hain't he at your place?"

Clark shook his head. "He's been missing a day a week for a month or more. This week he's missed two days in a row."

Alva stood straight and took a couple of steps toward Clark. Pete had agreed to work for old man Clark three days a week and that's what he had better be doing. She wanted to ask Clark more about Pete being absent from work, but remembered that a person's privacy was a sacred thing, especially when it was your privacy.

"I hate to complain, Mrs. Press, but a man can't stay home to help his wife when he's owing a man for land. He signed an agreement with me. I'd be hard put to do it, but I get the land back if he don't work three days a week until it's paid for. Now, I understand an emergency day once in a while, but it's becoming a habit that's getting worse."

Alva caught on quick and said, "I see what you're sayin' and it's a fact. It hain't right for a man to stay home helping his wife when he's got a job to do. I give you my word he won't be stayin' home helping me no more. I'll even go a step further. I know for a fact your wife hain't able to do nothin' for herself bein' she's got that rheumatism in her joints and all. What do you say that I come to your home once a week, clean the place and cook a good meal for the two of you? That way you could get paid off quicker for this here piece of land."

"What about your baby?" Clark asked sounding skeptical.

"This here baby don't slow me down none. You can see I've got him fixed where he can sleep right on while I work."

Clark looked at her for a long moment until things settled clearly in his head. He had a strong suspicion he'd be taking the land back if he didn't do as this woman asked. She'd bring Pete in to work and see that he was there every day he was supposed to be there. Pete couldn't sneak off from her if she was where she could watch him.

He held out his hand.

She placed her hand in his and they shook. He felt her calluses and a strength that matched his own.

"You got a deal," Clark said. "Your work day will count the same as Pete's work day. He left there wishing he could trade Pete for her. He'd met a lot of women in his time, but none exactly like Alva Press.

Alva carefully put away her hoe and precious seeds before she went searching for Pete. She found him lying in the shade down by the creek, asleep. His eyes flew open as he was bodily picked up off the ground and flung into the deepest part of the water. It wasn't deep enough to keep stars from flashing through the black part of his brain when his head hit rock on the bottom of the creek bed. He came up, coughing and sputtering, trying to catch his breath. Water poured out of his mouth as he scuttled to the creek bank. He sank to his knees, heaving up the packed lunch he had eaten before he fell asleep.

Alva stood on the bank watching Pete. Jay was still in his makeshift papoose sleeping against the muscled softness of his mother's body. He had been no hindrance to her when she picked Pete up off the ground. Anger had pumped adrenaline through her body like the throbbing of a boil. She waited now; ready to take his head off if he wanted to fight her. She knew a little man, like a banty rooster, could be scrappy, but she wasn't scrappy. She was all business and business was to straighten this man out once and for all.

A banty rooster of a man wasn't too scrappy when he had been knocked nearly cold and half drowned. When he finished puking, he rolled over on his back and looked up through the pale green buds of the trees at the blue of the sky. Shock was settling in on him as he realized she had thrown him like a rock.

"She hain't human," he said as he shivered there in the dirt.

"You told old man Clark you was stayin' home to help me. You best be gettin' yourself home where you're gonna help me till it's pitch black night."

He got to his feet and made sure he kept a good distance ahead of her. It would take a bigger fool than he was to fight with her when he was this near killed.

Chapter 12

Alva had never seen anything like the Clark house on the inside. She had passed by the outside and always looked at it with wonder. How did folks ever come up with money to build a house out of brick, especially a two-story house? She figured they had to cheat all kinds of people in a bad way. Yet, since she had been working for Clark, she was beginning to wonder about the cheating part. She had seen nothing but honesty and straightforward truth in him and his sad little wife.

Mattie Clark had rheumatoid arthritis so bad it put her to bed. Most every move she made caused her pain. Doctors tried to keep her doped up on pain medicine, but it didn't work too well.

"If you was to mix up Epsom salt and kerosene and rubbed on your joints it would give you a bit of ease," Alva told her.

Mattie's thin face twisted into a frown. "I better not," she said. Although, she would try almost anything to ease her pain.

"I see." Alva looked down on her lying in bed. The store-bought sheets were white and smooth, with one on the bottom and another, unheard of waste to Alva, on the top. A quilt in pale pink shades was hand stitched with delicate design and covered with a lace bedspread. "You'd rather lie there and suffer than mess up your fancy bedding with kerosene?"

"I guess you're right about that," Mattie admitted. "I like my pretty bed things. A person will never have anything if they don't take care of what they've already got."

"You could afford to buy more."

"Alva," Mattie said. "I'm a lot older than you, and I'm not real smart, but I've learned a few things during my life. Folks think we're rich because we have a few nice things, but they're wrong. We're not rich. The secret to having things, is working hard and smart. Once you get a thing, you take care of it and keep it forever. This bed and all the bedding were handed down to me by my mother. I've cared for them like they were a child."

"Was this house handed down too?"

"Yes. It was. Each generation tried to add something to it instead of taking away." Mattie wanted to tell her more. She wanted to tell Alva a man that was always drinking moonshine liquor never accomplished much. A woman that waited on her man hand and foot never accomplished much either. Accomplishments came when a man and a woman worked together toward a goal, but how did she explain her belief to a woman that had been raised way back in the hills of Hemlock Ridge? A woman that was steeped into the mountain tradition that the man was God and the woman a slave to him.

Alva wore a deep frown on her face as she spoke her thoughts. "My Maw han't even got her right mind to pass on. It was taken away by God only knows what. You ain't from these parts are you?"

"My parents came from Baltimore."

"Figures. Most northerners don't think like mountain folks. Mountain folks thank God if their belly is full and their skin is warm. They don't have the gall to demand God make the food delicious and the warmth a beautiful pleasure."

"Maybe they should," Mattie smiled her sweet smile at Alva. "God might understand."

"I've got my doubts about that. Now, if you get

in more pain than you can put up with, I'll carry you outside in the sun and lay you down on a pallet. The sun can bake in the kerosene and salt. Then I can put you in a wash tub of warm water before I stick you back in that pretty bed of yours."

Alva couldn't help laughing to herself when, in desperation, Mattie tried her suggestion. It gave Mattie enough ease until Mattie said she wished she could sleep in the concoction day and night, but Mattie still insisted things deserved special care if you wanted them to last.

After Alva finished hanging the wash on the line, she was looking at the brick on the outside of the Clark house. It wasn't mud that held them together.

"What has your attention?" old man Clark asked her as he came from the cabbage field and saw her fingering the brick.

"What's holdin' these bricks together?"

"Mortar."

"What's mortar?"

"It's like concrete. You mix it with sand and water."

"Would it hold rocks together better than mud?" Alva wanted to know.

"Yes it does, and you almost never have to

replace it. It's not like cinching with mud between logs and stone." Clark grinned at the young woman's curiosity. "I've got some bags of it in the shed."

"Could I take a look at that stuff?"

They went to the shed where there were at least twenty bags of mortar mix stored in the dry.

"Can you buy more of that stuff?" Alva wanted to know.

"Certainly."

"Let's make a deal. I'll work another day a week if you'll pay me a bag of mortar."

Clark nodded. He'd never had a worker that wanted to trade for mortar. He was anxious to see what this woman planned to do with it. "I'll give you two bags of mortar for each day you work extra."

This time, she held out her hand and Clark placed his big paw over hers in a handshake.

Chapter 13

Bobbie looked out the window to see Preacher Holloman show up, finding Maw sitting in the swept yard piling up little mounds of dirt. Maw's feet were bare and dirty. Her hair was hanging gray and uncombed over her shoulders and back. Bobbie saw a puzzled, sorrowful expression on his face. It faded some as he looked at Maw in bewilderment.

Bobbie came out onto the porch wishing she could make him disappear. She had enough problems the way things stood, unless this preacher could really perform miracles, cure the sick, or raise the dead.

"Come take yourself a chair on the porch, Preacher," she invited as she motioned her hand to one of the twine bottom chairs. "I'll fetch you a dipper of cold water if you want."

"Yeah, I'd like that," he said as he climbed up the steps and took the chair. He couldn't force his eyes away from Maw sitting in the dirt. "The last time I saw your maw was in the church house with a baby in her lap and her other children scattered about the benches. She was tall and dignified without one trace of dirt on her or her children. 'Cleanliness is next to Godliness,' she told me many a time, now look at her playing in the yard like a two year old."

Bobbie didn't move.

"Zoe, ha Zoe Dyke," he said over-loud. "It's me, Preacher Holloman. You know me, don't you?"

Zoe stared, as though she were transfixed at something.

She was seeing a snake crawling in the grass not five feet from her.

It's all right Zoey girl," her pa was telling her. "You don't have to be afeard of a little ole grass snake. It won't hurt you none." She kept hearing the words "It won't hurt you none," over and over. She believed her pa, but still, she couldn't move. She was paralyzed to the spot.

Bobbie turned her back on the preacher, went inside, and retuned with water in a glass.

He took the glass from her hand and looked at her sweet, childish face. "Nobody told me about the state of affairs you got here. Reckon folks wanted to spare me while I'm deep in my own sorrow. I'll never recover from the departure of my dear Ester. God rest her righteous soul." He made a point of clearing his throat. "Looks like Zoe Dyke turned into a mumbling idiot."

Bobbie clenched her teeth for a few moments before she was able to speak.

"Maw ain't herself, yet. She's in need of your prayers for I reckon only God can help her." Bobbie sat down on the chair from the preacher. She didn't like being close to him. The way he looked at her made her skin crawl. It was the same way he looked at her each Sunday in the church house.

He cleared his throat again and drank the water, all of it. His eyes took in the white skin of Bobbie's legs and bare feet. He looked at the slender softness of her arms and hands as she took the glass from him and sat it down on the porch plank.

"How long has she been this away?"

"Since Lacy was birthed." She took a breath of air. "I hated it about your wife and all. I've never had a chance to tell you that."

"Thank you," he said as he looked at her delicate face, again. "You're nothing like most mountain women. You're a lot like my Ester."

Bobbie was silent.

Several of the boys ran through the yard. None of them came close their Maw. Preacher Holloman looked beyond Maw to the steep hill behind the barn where somebody was trying to plow the steep ground with a horse.

"That Alvin?"

"It hain't Pap. It's Clayton. He hain't got the knack of plowin 'yet. Reckon a thing takes time to learn."

"Where is Alvin?"

"He went off through the woods huntin' game for supper. I've kilt off the chickens till there hain't no more left to kill." She didn't feel bad about lying to him. It was better than telling him Pap was in bed drunker than a mash bloated hog. It was better than him sitting there wanting her to fix him a chicken dinner just because he showed up near mealtime. She only had three hens and a rooster left, and she had to keep them alive if she wanted eggs to eat and to set for hatching. He had only himself to feed. She had to feed thirteen hungry bellies three times a day.

"Some of them boys ought to be capable of getting a lot of work done. How old are they, anyhow?"

"Clayton's twelve, Dean's eleven and Evert's ten. The others han't big enough to help much. Course Frank, Grady and Haverty can do some. The others are just little. Maw's baby was a girl. I named her Lacy." She thought a preacher ought to know folks names, but she reckoned it wasn't a matter of importance to him.

"Won't be long till Alvin can set back and take it easy with that many boys. Ester, God rest her soul, was never able to give me a boy to help me with work."

Bobbie never said a thing that came to her mind.

Preacher Holloman left with a hungry belly and hungry eyes as he looked back at Bobbie standing on the porch. A preacher needed him a wife to help him out and do the work around the house. He needed one that could cook and one that didn't get old before her time. Bobbie might do, but the look of her maw sitting in the dirt was enough to make a man worry. He consoled himself with the thought that a just God could send a Preacher a way to ease his sorrow without sending him a wife.

He stopped at the Jones place just as Sarrie Jones was placing her family's dinner on the table. She hurriedly opened another can of beans and a can of corn. Thank goodness she had baked a large pone of cornbread in hopes it would be enough for supper, which it wouldn't be now. Everybody knew how much food the Preacher could put down his throat.

"Welcome, Preacher," she said with a smile of greeting, but her heart wasn't in it. She wished she had the nerve to sic Jack, the Shepherd dog, on him. But folks with proper raising always welcomed the Preacher, no matter who he was or when he showed up.

"It's an honor to have you show up to share a meal with us," she said as she smoothed her work apron and pinned her bun of hair more securely to the back of her head. Besides, God might not take too kindly if she had too harsh thoughts about a preacher. There was just something about the spiritual world that common folks didn't understand and had to be careful with.

"Now, hain't it a shame about Mrs. Dyke," the Preacher said after his first few mouthfuls of food.

"How's that?" Harrison Jones asked.

"Her mind and all. It hurt my heart to see her playin' in the dirt like a baby. Why, she never did know I was right there in front of her eyes."

"What a shame. We hadn't heard a word and us livin' right next door." Harrison considered a mile through the woods next door. "Sarrie, you'll have to go by and check on her."

"So that's why she hain't been to meetings for a spell," Sarrie said. "I just thought she hadn't gotten her strength back yet. What was her last youngun anyway?"

"A girl." He recalled hearing Bobbie say.

Sarrie Jones shook her head in a gesture of pity. It wasn't going to be easy on that remaining girl with her Maw out of order. A pile of boys weren't much help around the house, and God knew what that Alvin Dyke was like. She reckoned she ought to walk over there and check on things after a while.

Sarrie Jones wasn't one to sit on her hind end and think on things once she got a notion in her head. She went to the Dyke house as soon as the preacher left and the dishes were done. She found Bobbie trying to feed everybody on little more than poke sallet, branch lettuce, and potatoes, skin and all. She knew Bobbie didn't peel the potatoes because she had too few to waste peelings. Sarrie went straight to Maw and placed her hand on her forehead.

"Bobbie Dyke, who cared for your Maw during childbirth?" Sarrie asked.

"Alva did."

Sarrie nodded. "Your maw's done developed

childbed fever. It's affected her brain. She'll have to have some powerful medicine to get her well. Then it'll take a long spell. I've seen this before."

"Where do I get the medicine?" Bobbie wanted to know.

"From a real doctor, if there was one to be had. Until then, I'll do what I can to help." Sarrie didn't need to ask Bobbie why nobody came to ask for her help during childbirth, after all she did serve as midwife for Hemlock Ridge. Zoe Dyke had given birth alone to all but her three first children. Alvin Dyke didn't think she should need help any longer. He said a woman that was any account a tall should know what to do after a count of three. He added that Zoey's path was well greased. Sarrie could hate him for that alone, but there was a lot more than that to hate about Alvin Dyke.

"The Preacher prayed for her," Bobbie said because she couldn't think of anything else to say.

"That bucket won't carry much water."

"What?"

"Never mind, child. I'm just talkin' to hear my head rattle." Sarrie looked from the floor where Zoe was sitting next to the bed where Alvin lay passed out drunk. Least he hadn't eaten up part of their sparse dinner. To her way of thinking, Alvin Dyke didn't deserve the food he ate. If God was truly just, Alvin would stagger out the door never to be seen again. She just didn't know why there had to be men like Alvin Dyke. She guessed it was the same reason there had to be copperhead snakes. To make a person careful what they grabbed a hold of.

"How's the baby doin'?" Sarrie looked about but didn't see the baby.

"All right. I've got her a pallet behind the cook stove. She's so little I've got to keep her extra warm."

Sarrie went from the front room to the kitchen and looked on the feather pillow. A tiny baby was asleep. "If you want, I can take her home with me." Sarrie offered.

"No," Bobbie said quickly. "I feed her on a bottle. Besides, I take her to Alva almost every day. Alva's got plenty of milk. She's so little she needs human milk."

"Zoe don't have milk then?"

"Nary a drop."

"It's a good thing," Sarrie told her. "Milk from a woman with childbed fever could kill a baby right fast."

Bobbie looked at Sarrie, wide-eyed and,

grateful that God had the wisdom not to let Maw give milk.

"Sarrie," Bobbie's forehead was wrinkled with worry. "Where have you seen another woman with childbed fever?"

"It's been a good while back. It was when my own granny was a midwife. She taught me about the ways of medicine, you know. I followed at her heels and she taught me right good. It was over Pond Mountain at the head of Soup Bean Creek. Your momma reminds me a lot of that woman."

Sarrie stopped talking and began to think. Yes, the woman reminded her a lot of Zoe in several ways. A house full of younguns, run-down by over-work, desperation, and a near starvation diet of wrinkled potatoes.

"Did she get over it?" Bobbie interrupted Sarrie's thoughts.

"As far as I know, she did. Can't recall hearin' much about her after that."

Within a few days, Sarrie and every other woman in Hemlock Ridge was bringing herbs and food. Some of the women brought medicine a doctor had given them at some time or the other. A couple of the bottles of medicine, Sarrie allowed Bobbie to give her Maw. Men brought sacks of shriveled potatoes they had left over from winter and weren't going to plant. Women brought their old cans of vegetables that should have been emptied years before. Bobbie was glad to get the extra food and promised to save their empty canning jars for them to pick up sometime. One man brought her three bushels of corn to plant. None offered to help Clayton with the plowing. That should have been Alvin Dyke's job. He didn't have childbed fever.

"What's wrong with you?" Alva demanded of Bobbie when she found out what folks were doing. "Hain't you got no pride? I'd rather starve to death than take people's leftovers. You know good and well Maw wouldn't allow for other peoples charity."

Bobbie smiled softly as she watched Lacy suck her fill of Alva's milk. "I hain't willin' to watch my baby brothers starve just to save my own pride. Maw just didn't put up enough food last year. Besides, Maw don't know nothing about charity. She don't even know she's still alive."

Alva nodded in satisfaction. Guess Maw found out how much work she did around the place. When she married Pete, it took more than half Maw's help away. Bobbie couldn't replace her.

Bobbie wasn't nothing but a spindly slip of a girl. Too much like Maw.

"You could take Pap's liquor away and tell him he has to get out there and do some work," Alva said.

"I wish you'd come over and tell him that. You have more strength and determination more than the rest of us put together."

Alva wondered if she was to take that as a compliment. Finally, she decided it was a compliment. Pap would have been a fine man if it wasn't for his crazy temper and his love for liquor. When a boy started guzzling that stuff at an early age, it got a powerful hold on him, a hold that wouldn't turn loose. But, she didn't rush home with Bobbie to straighten Pap out. Instead, when Bobbie left, Alva grabbed the pick and shovel and started digging out a foundation beside her sapling and mud one-room house.

Old man Clark told her every house needed a good foundation. He had let her borrow a book on such things, but she was having a hard time understanding it.

Old man Clark grinned when she asked him if he would allow her and Pete to clear all the rocks off his land that joined their meager five acres. He said he would give her a few extra bags of mortar for their work. Alva knew he wanted to see what kind of rock house she could make herself, or bully Pete into making. Alva knew Clark had the cleanest house he had lived in since Mattie got sick. She knew she was broader than a garden gate was wide, but her size didn't slow her down. She could put out some work. She knew old man Clark was pleased.

Chapter 14

Bobbie's hands shook so badly she could hardly open the barn door. Her whole body was on fire with pain and sorrow. Why, oh, why had she followed Pap out to the barn? He wouldn't have really set the barn on fire. He was just drunk and wild out of his head. He didn't know what he was saying or what he was doing. Didn't he keep calling her Zoe when he attacked her after she took the lantern away from him and blew out the flame to keep him from throwing it into the hay?

He drank bad liquor. Swore it was eating a hole in the pit of his stomach. Demanded milk to ease the pain, but there was no milk. The cow was to calf in two weeks, and Bobbie had been forced to turn her dry. Pap said he aimed to burn the barn down. He said there was no reason to have a barn if there wasn't a milking cow in it.

She begged a little milk from the neighbors whenever she could, but it wasn't enough. She had to brave Alva and her bad temper daily. Alva was in the family way again and it was safer to face an angry bull than Alva.

Dear God! She wished Pap had been an angry bull. She'd rather be dead than have done to her what he did.

She leaned her body into the door and felt it open as the cool of the night air hit. She gulped the air into her lungs and ran toward the creek behind the barn. The moon was high in the sky, but she didn't need the moonlight to find her way. She ran into the water, lying down on her back so the water ran over her body, slow and chilling. If only it was ten foot deep; if only it was swift enough to carry her away forever; if only she could just die and forever be gone from Hemlock Ridge. She cried and moaned like a wounded animal caught in a trap.

She had no idea how long she had lain in the water when she heard Clayton's voice calling her.

"Bobbie? Oh, Bobbie?"

Silent sobs shook her.

"Where you at, Bobbie? Lacy needs you."

Bobbie didn't want to bring herself back to this earth. She wanted to die there in the water, to never raise her body up and care for her siblings. So at first, she didn't answer Clayton. Not until she heard him going toward the barn.

"Clayton!" she yelled as she jumped up out of the water. "Over here! I'm over here."

She heard him coming toward her and met him on shaky legs that could barely walk.

"What are you doin' out here?

"I come to check on things." Her teeth chattered until she could hardly talk. "I fell in the creek."

"Fell in the creek?" His voice sounded of disbelief. "How'd you do a thing like that? Checkin' on what?"

"No. Don't grab hold of me. You'll get all wet." Bobbie pushed his hands away and tried to stand straight. " What's wrong with Lacy?"

"She's cryin' hard and I can't get her to hush up."

"Go on back to her. I'm comin' as fast as I can."

"I shore hain't gonna leave you. Are you hurt somewhere? Can't I help you?"

"I'm fine. Just cold's all. I hain't hurt. No, I hain't hurt."

Clayton slowed his walking to match Bobbie's speed.

Bobbie fixed Lacy a bottle of potato water with honey in it. Poor little thing was hungry.

"You get yourself dried off. I'll give her the bottle," Clayton told her, as his sharp eyes looked her over. "You shore you're not hurt? You hain't lookin' right."

"I'm fine," she tried to sound fine. She wished to goodness she could blow out the kerosene lamp. She didn't want Clayton looking at her when she was like this. How was it they didn't have food enough to eat and they still had kerosene for the lamp? "Did Lacy wake up the boys?"

"No. They're all in the loft sleepin' like logs. She only woke me and I knew you were gone when you didn't get her."

"Good. No need for the boys to be woke up." She left him with Lacy while she went to her pallet in the corner of the kitchen, next to the long table. She no longer slept in the loft with the boys. There just wasn't enough room for her to lie down.

She had to put on her Sunday dress, until she could get her everyday dress washed and dried tomorrow. But it couldn't be helped. Once she was dried off, she sent Clayton back to bed and rocked the fretful Lacy to sleep.

Bobbie cried until dawn was getting ready to break. Before it was light out, she headed through the woods toward Alva's. She didn't care how hateful Alva had become. Little Lacy had to have enough milk to live. It just wasn't right that Alva refused to keep Lacy during the night and feed her like she did Jay. Of course Jay was her own boy, but Lacy was her sister. Bobbie understood Alva worked mighty hard. She worked for old man Clark, did up her own work plus she was building herself a rock house. Alva wouldn't have been able to keep Lacy during the day. Bobbie understood that. Still, during the night, it would have been better on Lacy than feeding her honey water.

Alva took one look at Bobbie and looked again. "What in tarnation happened to you? You look like a mule dragged you down a rocky holler."

"I fell down the bank and rolled into the creek."

"Well, quit moonin' around lookin' so pitiful. You hain't the first and you won't be the last to get skinned up."

That's true, Bobbie thought. It sure was true enough. Girls had this sort of thing done to them all the time. Only this time it happened to be her. She hung her head and couldn't help looking pitiful.

"I'll stop botherin' you soon as the cow calves. Broth boiled outta taters don't seem to do Lacy no good. She cries a lot for milk and I don't have none to give her. I got no other choice than bring her to you."

"Humph." Alva gave her normal snort. All this aggravation was part her own fault. She could have let Maw and Lacy die. Probably would have been the best thing she could have done, but like an idiot, she kept them alive so Maw could sit in the dirt and blubber like a moron, while Lacy cried and shriveled up like an old woman.

She unbuttoned three middle buttons of the man's shirt she was wearing and let her heavy breast tumble out. Lacy sucked like there had never been anything as good.

"You might as well eat a biscuit and gravy. You look like you could use a bite of food yourself. You've fell away to the boneyard. I reckon you've been starvin' yourself and givin' the others your share. Hain't the folks totin' you food no more?"

"Clayton and I've got a big garden planted. It just hain't come on yet. We've got peas and onions and lettuce we've been eatin on."

"I knew they'd stop carryin' you food once they figured they'd done their Christian duty. Have you noticed goodwill only lasts until it becomes inconvenient?"

"I didn't expect folks to help forever."

"And Pap's still dog drunk hain't he?"

Bobbie downed her head. She couldn't talk about him right now. She couldn't even make herself think about him. She'd think later when time had passed and she was stronger.

"He still pokin' on Maw? She could have another youngun, you know, even the way she is. You tearin' rags for her every month?"

"Please, don't talk about that," Bobbie begged.

"I take it old Sarrie Jones han't cured Maw's childbed fever as she calls what Maw has. Don't take just one biscuit. Put three or four on your plate. Cover 'em good with gravy and eat 'em while I watch you. Don't want you fallin' over dead from starvation. I've got no intention takin' on that motley crowd after they kill you off. I've got another boy crawlin' around in my belly, and I don't have time fur nobody else."

"Maw ain't able to do nothin. She just sits lookin' off in her eyes while she laughs and mumbles. I've about give up hope she'll get better."

"She don't want to get better. She likes it right where she is."

Bobbie couldn't see how that was true, but she had no intention of arguing with Alva. She needed Alva's milk and she sure to goodness needed the biscuits and gravy she was eating.

"How do you know it's a boy?" Bobbie asked.

"Cause I need me some help around this place. Pete hain't much of a man, so I'll grow me some boys that are."

"I got Clayton," Bobbie said. "He makes the boys weed the garden and the corn patch. We planted a lot more taters than Maw ever planted. Nearly everybody brought us taters."

"Bet that's what you been livin' on. You, the boys, and the hogs eatin' folks' thrown away taters."

She didn't tell Alva how glad she was to have those potatoes.

Pete came inside carrying a bucket of milk. He strained it and gave Bobbie a quart without asking Alva's permission.

"Old man Clark's got a Jersey milk cow he's a mind to sell. Why don't you send Clayton and a couple of the boys down to him? They could work out that cow if Clark is willin'," Pete told her.

Alva gave Pete a hard look, but she didn't say a word as she pulled Lacy from her breast and gave her back to Bobbie.

That evening Bobbie carried Lacy as she took Clayton, Dean, and Evert to old man Clark's place. She made them sit behind a rock in the woods on the opposite side of the house. The side away from the path Pete and Alva made walking to and from home.

"Why we sittin' here, Bobbie? Why don't we just walk on up there and ask him?" Clayton wanted to know.

"We best wait till Alva and Pete go on home. We don't want old man Clark thinking Alva put us up to this."

"Pete did," Clayton said.

"Nobody needs to know that, do they?"

The boys looked at her hard, but they didn't ask any more questions as they waited. It was good they had waited. Old man Clark was out in the fields working with Pete and a bunch of other men. Only Pete and Clark came all the way to the house. The other men walked off in different directions. Still, Bobbie wouldn't let them move until Pete, with Alva carrying Jay, were clean out of sight and out of hearing.

"Well, what do we have here?" Clark asked as he answered Bobbie's knock on the door.

"Heard you had a milk cow for sale?" Bobbie jiggled Lacy and tried to keep herself from shaking with nervousness. She'd never met old man Clark before and she'd certainly never tried to buy a cow.

"That I have," Clark said. "She's getting old and I've replaced her with a young heifer."

"Could you see fit to work these boys until they pay you for her?"

Clark looked at the boys. Their faces were clean, but their clothes and hands could use a washing. The girl looked clean enough as she held a baby that appeared to be days old. She had some bruises and scratches on her face, arms and legs. Her eyes were puffy as though she had been crying. He didn't miss seeing the bottle partway filled with water she held in her hand. He didn't need to ask. He could tell by the looks of them that food was not something they saw much of. And that poor little baby couldn't live on water.

"You boys good workers?" Clark asked, wondering how they knew he was considering selling the cow.

"Mister, we're the best they is." The oldest boy reared back and lifted his head at a proud angle. "There hain't a weed in Bobbie's garden, the tater patch, or the corn field."

"I reckon you boys know that I grow corn, beans, cabbage, tomatoes and other produce for the market. I have weeding and hoeing that needs to be done. So I reckon we could strike a deal." He held his hand out to Clayton.

Clayton wiped his hand on his britches before he shook with Clark. The other two boys did the same.

"Thank you," Bobbie said. "They'll be here tomorrow at sun up."

"Wait a minute," Clark stopped them as they started to walk away. "Make it about seven o'clock in the morning. Sun up's a little early for an old man like me. Follow me up to the barn and you can lead the cow home."

"We hain't worked her out yet," Clayton said.

"You will. No need for me to be milking her when I don't have to." He looked at Bobbie as they walked toward the barn. "How old is your baby?"

"She's three months old now. She was right little when she was born."

"Is she yours?"

"She's our sister."

Clark watched them leave leading the cow along the path Pete and Alva had worn slick. He had no doubt the boys would be there at seven to work out that Jersey cow. He just hoped there was plenty of grass where they were taking her.

"What kept you outside so long?" Mattie Clark asked her husband.

"Some kids came by wanting to trade work for a milk cow. I wanted to give them that cow, Mattie. But I knew I couldn't. You ruin people's pride when you give them something. Working your finger to the bone for the things you need makes you stand tall and proud at the end of the day."

Chapter 15

The boys showed up the next morning while old man Clark was eating his breakfast. The two smaller boys stood behind Clayton as he knocked on the kitchen door. Clark opened the door and looked down on the three boys. Each was wearing bibbed overalls with no shirt underneath.

"We're here," Clayton said as though he was proud of his announcement.

"So I see. It's not seven o'clock yet."

"Oh. We hain't got no timepiece. Maw's quit workin' and Bobbie couldn't fix it."

Clark started to tell them to wait on the porch for him, but the hollow look of them wouldn't let him. Besides, boys didn't work well on empty bellies. And he did intend for these three boys to work out their cow.

"You boys come on inside and set down at the table."

Clayton walked across the kitchen floor and sat down on the chair Clark indicated. His eyes were the size of a quarter and his mouth hung open. Never in his life had he seen such a place. The floor was covered in some fancy looking stuff that shined like a wet rock. A concrete trough was running down one side of the wall and it was actually full of running water. The biggest cook stove he'd ever seen was against the wall giving off heat, and the smells coming from it made him swallow several times. He held his hands in his lap, afraid to touch the white lace cloth on the table. He looked at his brothers to make sure they weren't rubbing the white cloth, getting it dirty. They had scrunched up like they didn't know what to do next.

"Boys, I was just fixing me a bite of breakfast. I'd be honored if you ate with me."

A longing look came to all three faces, but Clayton spoke up. "Bobbie fed us some before we left home. We wouldn't want to put you out."

Disappointment flashed across the other boys' faces. Clark almost grinned but didn't. Mountain pride whipped into a boy at an early age would make him starve rather than admit he was hungry. Clark respected that pride.

"It won't put me out because I'm being selfish. I've worked men for over forty years. I get more work out of my men if I feed them a hardy breakfast."

It occurred to Clayton to ask why the rest of his workers weren't there eating, but the smell of bacon and eggs Clark was frying in a pan stopped him.

Clark gave them each two fried eggs, two slices of bacon, and a biscuit covered in gravy. The boys wolfed it down like starved dogs.

"We'll come back at dinner time and eat a big meal. Alva doesn't work today, but she left a big pot of beans, hog meat, and potatoes from supper last night. We can warm it up and eat fine." He saw eagerness in the boys' eyes.

Pete and two other men used mules to cultivate the row crops while Clark and the three boys chopped weeds and hoed up fresh dirt around the plants. Clark could tell the boys knew what hoeing was about, but they were bone tired when dinnertime came. Their bare feet dragged in the dirt as they walked from the field to the house.

"You boys not tired are you?" Clark couldn't resist asking them. He liked to see people tired from hard work. Especially boys. He believed hard work made a man out of a boy, fast.

"No sir." All three said at the same time.

The youngest boy looked up at him with wide eyes. "How long does a body have to work for a cow?"

Clayton poked him in the ribs with his elbow.

"That's a fair question. Most men like to bring finances right up on top. Let's see now, a good milk cow can bring as much as thirty dollars."

The boys had never heard tell of that much money. Clayton figured they'd be working for Clark the rest of their lives.

"But like I told you, this cow is old."

Actually she was a little beyond her prime but she wasn't old for a milk cow, and she had been bred to his fine Jersey bull four months before, right after she calved. He sold the bull calf as veal. Milk cows produced mighty fine veal.

"I reckon ten dollars would be a fair enough deal. Do you think you three boys can do the work of one grown man?"

"I'm pert near growed," Clayton informed Clark.

"Pert near is not all the way. I was right your age not too mighty long ago. I remember it well, but I don't long to be back there. Growing pains. I had them when I was a boy. Had them bad." He made a face like he remembered the hurt. "You three boys can earn the same as a man. Ten cents a day until you've paid her off."

Clark watched Clayton try to figure out how long that would take, but Clayton finally gave it up. Clark knew the longer he worked these boys, the more he could teach them. The more they learned the better chance at life they would have. Too bad he didn't have another cow to sell them.

"How many brothers and sisters do you boys have?"

The two youngest remained silent, willing for their older brother to do all the talking.

"There's nine of us boys and three girls."

"Twelve." Clark opened the kitchen door and let the boys enter. He'd known a family that had twenty children. They all pitched in and helped out. Did well for themselves. "What does your pa do?"

Clayton was silent so long the youngest finally said something.

"Drinks liquor." The youngest got another jab in the ribs from Clayton.

"What's his name?"

"Alvin Dyke."

Clark thought he had heard that name before, but he couldn't remember where right at the moment.

"What about your mother?" Clark knew he was walking ground that was none of his business, but he wanted to find out more about these boys.

"Maw's name is Zoe and she's not doin' so good since Lacy was birthed," Clayton said.

"Lacy was the little baby your sister was carrying yesterday?"

"Yeah, sir," Clayton frowned. "If'n you want to know so all fired much, why don't you just come on home with us and have a look for yourself?"

Clark nodded his head as he lit a fire in the stove to warm their dinner. "Sorry son. I didn't mean to stick my nose so far into your business."

"I reckon hit's all right," Clayton said. "Reckon rich folks want to know what poor folks live like."

Clark turned to the boy. The boy's blue eyes were sparkling with intelligence. His skinny body oozed pride and determination. This boy would grow up and make something out of himself if he had half a chance. Clark knew if he could, he would help give him that half chance.

Clark knew education wasn't easy. It came in many different forms and was steeped in many different disguises. School learning was a form that was hard to come by. There were too few schools in the mountains and too few reasons to attend. Knowing correct verbage didn't make it any easier to hoe a row of corn. Take Mattie, his beloved wife. She had a college education and never did a thing with it. She ended up a farmer's wife. Clark wondered often if his life would have been different if he had been the one with a college education instead of Mattie.

"Rich is a matter of interpretation," Clark said, more to himself than the boys. "Just because a man has a few material things and a little money don't make him rich."

Clayton gave Clark a look that told Clark the boy didn't believe a word Clark had said. Rich in the mountains was the elusive word that pertained to anyone that had just a little more than you.

"Rich is a matter of eatin' or not eatin'," Clayton said and wished he hadn't. He didn't want anybody to know food was scarce in their house.

"In that case we're all rich right now." Clark grinned as he dished up bowls of food and set it on the table in front of the boys. Alva had left more food than he and Mattie could eat in several days time, but he knew why she cooked so much. Alva ate the leftovers.

Alva was put out when she discovered there weren't any leftovers. But she solved that problem easy enough. She cooked more.

Mattie was a thin little woman who didn't eat much, but she had some strict food requirements. She wanted little to no grease in her diet and very little sugar or salt. However, Clark was the opposite. He loved the greasy food Alva cooked, and salt was his manna.

"You got gall bladder problems," Alva told Mattie. "Folks what can't eat grease allus do."

"You may be right," Mattie agreed as she leaned heavily on Alva as Alva walked her toward a washtub of hot water. Her legs hurt bad. Her joints were extra swollen and painful today. Mattie was convinced Alva's hot water and Epsom salt bath helped ease her pain to a point of nearly endurable.

"I'll go strip some willow bark and brew you some tea while you soak in the water." Alva told Mattie as she helped lower her into the tub. "You can pour more honey in it to take away the bitterness. Instead of layin' up in bed so much, you outta get out and about more. Pain gets a good hold on you when you give in to it. Only way to whip pain is to work it to death. Never let it rest in you. If it rests, it may never let go."

Mattie did hate the taste of willow tea but it made her rest better, she had to admit. Her life had been a lot more comfortable since Alva arrived. But, she didn't agree that she needed to work her rheumatism instead of resting it in bed. Working her rheumatism was nothing short of torture and she was the first to admit she didn't have the grit and determination of a mountain woman like Alva. She was happy to remain a timid Baltimore city woman that liked her comfort whenever she was able to get it.

Alva brewed the tea, let Jay suck, and watched Mattie soak in the tub. She wondered how it was a useless woman like Mattie ended up marrying a capable man like old man Clark. She was convinced a man like Clark could have owned most of the county if he'd married a woman like herself. One with enough gumption to get somewhere in life. Strange it was, how a man like Clark got a woman like Mattie, and she got a man like Pete.

"Alva, I almost forgot to tell you Clark said to cook extra for lunch today. He's been feeding those boys breakfast and lunch."

Alva thought it was funny the way Mattie called dinner lunch, then called supper dinner. Baltimore women were uppity in their speech and ways. "What boys?"

"Boys from upon Hemlock Ridge. You probably know them. Clark said their last names are Dyke. They are working out payment for a milk cow."

Alva gritted her teeth and turned her back on Mattie. So that's why Bobbie hadn't showed up begging milk for Lacy. She should have known this would happen. It was all Pete's fault. He suggested it to Bobbie. She'd heard him herself, and she'd like to knock his teeth down his throat for opening his big mouth. She'd never had a thing in life, not one comfort, not one grain of food, not one single moment to herself that her parents or bothers and sister hadn't tried to take from her. With the Clarks, she was having it good. She was getting her a rock house built on land she was helping pay for. She had more than enough food to eat for the first time in her life, now her brothers had arrived at the Clark's ready to take it from her. If they ruined this for her, she aimed to flat out kill Pete Press. She sure enough would.

"You don't mind feedin' an extra bunch of mouths?" Alva asked.

"Goodness no. It's you that will do the cooking and the cleaning up. And the good Lord knows Clark has plenty of produce that's bruised and can't be sold. You know, above all things, Clark is a farmer. A mighty fine farmer if I do say so myself. He went to school, and he still reads books on how to increase production. He knows how to feed left over vegetation to cattle, hogs, and chickens. He then takes the manure the animals leave and spreads it on the land to produce more and better row crops to sell at the markets. Why, he even read that the Chinese and Japanese people use human waste as fertilizer for their own food.

"Clark believes people are spending too much of their time concentrating on feeding themselves. He says if food production was increased, food would be cheaper, and people could spend time improving their lives. He says there are inventions out there that has never been thought about."

Alva didn't comment. Pap never spread a shovel of manure on anything and neither did Maw, and she didn't really know what an invention was. She'd have to think on this a while.

Chapter 16

"**M**aw," Bobbie said out loud as she took a rag and fastened it to the material of Maw's bloomers with large safety pins. "Oh Maw, I don't know what to do,"

Maw looked at the far wall.

"Maw, can't you please come on back. I need you bad." She pulled Maw's bloomers up over her hips.

Maw laid there, her eyes open, breathing. Bobbie smoothed Maw's dress down to her knees.

"I'm afeard. Awfully afeard. I han't got nobody but you. Can't you come on back?" Bobbie pulled a sheet, the one with the hogs face, over Maw.

"What can I do to bring you back?" Bobbie looked at her a minute longer then left the room.

Clayton was standing on the porch. His face twisted with worry. "What are you afeard of, Bobbie?"

A shudder went through her body. What had she said? Not too much, she hoped. She hadn't known Clayton was listening.

"I'm afeard Maw will never be any better," she answered quickly.

"Hain't there airy thing we can do to help her? Old man Clark says if there's a will, there's a way."

Bobbie read the desperation in Clayton's face and knew he felt as helpless as she did. "Maybe if we had a real doctor to give her medicine. Otherwise, I reckon there just hain't much a body can do about nothing."

Bobbie stepped off the porch and went to the barn. She was tired, stoop shouldered and bent at the age of thirteen.

Bobbie tried to deny what she knew for a fact, but only for a little while. There was no way she was going to lie to herself. A body might as well face the truth and do what had to be done. The trouble was she didn't know what had to be done.

She always tore rags for herself each month for the past two years as regular as the passing of time. She tore rags this month too, but she hadn't used one. After another week passed, she knew she wasn't going to need rags for a while. Still, she waited and hoped.

Bobbie carried a bucket as she walked to the edge of the cow pasture. There, in the pasture were two cows. The fine Jersey milk cow she called Clarkie and the old brindle cow with her heifer calf. There was plenty of milk, Lacy wasn't hungry and Maw was still alive. She should be thankful, but there was no thankfulness in her as she bent over to pick wild strawberries. She capped the first handful and put them in her mouth. The taste was heaven, pure, sweet heaven.

When she puked them up, she knew for certain what was going on. She could hope no longer.

"Dear God, no!" she mumbled as she hung her head and wiped her mouth on her dress tail. Unwanted tears came to her eyes.

She let herself cry for a while, but only a while. She picked every berry she could find and went back to the house. No need to waste her strength on crying. Tears wouldn't help a thing. Lord in Heaven, what would help her, now?

She washed herself, the boys and Lacy real good Saturday night. She cleaned and pressed their clothes with the hot iron early Sunday morning. She had a need to look her best at the meeting house. There were several boys that attended church, but she couldn't recall one of them looking at her. Maybe that was because she never wanted one, or needed one. Today was different.

"Clayton, Dean, I expect you to care for the boys and make them behave inside. Do you want me to take Kyle?"

"No," Clayton said. "You care for Lacy. I'll take Kyle and Dean can hold Jarred."

Bobbie took her usual place beside Alva on the church bench. She let her arm touch her sister's arm—wanting to draw strength from her. Alva was strong, and tough, and capable. Bobbie needed those feelings. She needed someone to hold onto, someone stronger than herself.

For a moment, she considered telling Alva what had happened until she imagined Alva's voice, Alva's reaction. Alva would blame her. Tell her she should have fought harder, run faster, never gone to the barn after Pap in the first place. Pap wouldn't have outdone Alva. Alva had a right arm as powerful as the hind leg of a mule.

Bobbie looked at her own right arm. It was narrow and bony. It strained just to carry a full bucket of milk. Even ten-year-old Evert was stronger than she was. There was no fight in her, no outdoing Pap.

Hurt rose from her belly upward to settle in her throat and lie there and ache. She knew she couldn't tell anyone, not even Alva. Once people knew, what would they think of her? What would they think of Pap and the rest of her family? Dear God! She shuddered.

She took quick glances at the right hand side of the church. Older men sat in the front. Younger ones were in the back. Boys her age were on the last row, but they were too young. A husband needed to be at least seventeen. There was one twenty year old, Brackston Phillips. Brackston wouldn't make a good husband or father, but there was a chance he could be had.

All the girls stayed away from him. His mind came and went ever since he bragged how much liquor he could drink down his gullet at one time.

Folks said he did an admirable job until he passed out. He stayed passed out for nearly a week. Once he come to, he was never right again. Folks said he was as docile and gentle as a kitten at times. Then, for no apparent reason, he would go wild as a buck. His daddy had to run him down, drag him home, and hog-tie him up to a post made for that purpose.

Bobbie didn't think she would ever be strong enough to hog-tie Brackston Phillips.

There were Bo and Jackson Hinkle, brothers about sixteen or seventeen. Bo, the older, was fairly nice. Jackson was in the know-it-all, smart-ass stage. Bobbie feared the stage had set in with a permanent stay. The few other boys were just too young.

Lacy whimpered and Bobbie looked away from the right hand side as she gave Lacy her bottle. There was one advantage to bottle-feeding. She didn't have to leave the meetinghouse or suffer the embarrassment of pulling out a teat as Alva had done that time. Bobbie knew it wasn't something Alva normally did. Alva had a lot of pride about herself, and she was sensitive to what people thought. Alva was just mad cause the preacher woke Jay up and made him cry.

Bobbie looked up from Lacy and saw Preacher Holloman watching her as he preached his sermon. She dropped her eyes fast; afraid he would come to her again, beseeching her to be saved. A slight rumble came from Alva's throat. Bobbie knew Alva saw the look the preacher was giving her.

When the meeting was over and the crowd headed home, Bobbie made sure she bumped into Bo Hinkle.

"Oh, I'm sorry," she said as sweetly as she knew how.

Bo eyed her hard and long.

"Bo. You best hurry to the creek and wash that arm real good. A crazy, no account Dyke just rubbed herself on you," Jackson laughed like he had made a funny joke.

Bo brushed at his shirtsleeve and walked off. "She musta thought I was you." He gave his brother a hard shove on the shoulder as they hurried away.

Alva saw what happened, and heard what was said. She came to Bobbie's side and said low enough not to be overheard.

"You stay away from them boys. They hain't fit for nothin'. Stay away from that preacher too. He's the one to watch out for. He's used to pokin' often. Reckon he's done built up a pile of blue balls. He'd poke you quicker'n he'd eat chicken."

Alva walked away from Bobbie to the bridge where Bo and Jackson were throwing rocks in the middle of the creek. Her body, wide and massive, managed to bump into both boys just right, knocking them off the side of the bridge into the water.

"You confounded, no account Hinkle boys! You best watch who you bump into," Alva hollered down at them loud enough to be heard throughout the valley. Folks had better learn not to mess with her or her kin.

For the first time ever, Bobbie realized why Alva was the way she was.

Alva knew what people living on Hemlock Ridge thought about a Dyke.

Now, Bobbie knew.

There would be no good husband for her, ever. She was one of the crazy, no-good Dykes, and she was about to make the name of Dyke even worse.

"God," Bobbie prayed. "Tell me what to do. I'll do anything, just please, please tell me what."

For the better part of a week, Bobbie prayed. She believed if she prayed hard enough and long enough, God would hear her and provide an answer.

In the first part of a long night, she woke up in a cold sweat. She had a nightmare. She sat up and raked her hands over her face as she recalled the nightmare in detail. Her breath quickened and she trembled all over. It was a nightmare all right. One where God told her what she was to do.

The moon was high in the night sky by the time she gathered enough courage to do what God told her. She picked Lacy up off the floor and wrapped a towel around her. She couldn't take a chance on

Lacy waking the boys while she was gone. She got the bottle, filled it with milk and slipped out the door.

The night was cool, but the wind was gentle and soft as though it was trying to give her comfort while she walked through the woods. Trees cast shadows and bullfrogs sang in the swampy ground along the creek banks. Stars filled the sky and the moon shined with a brightness that only happened on occasion.

"See," Bobbie whispered into the towel covering Lacy. "God's made it light enough for me to walk through these woods. He means for me to do this. If he didn't it'd be dark as pitch."

She would not be able to find her way through the woods, although she knew exactly where she was going.

"I gotta do this, Lacy. You know I have to. I hain't got no choice. I gotta do this. You understand that, don't you. I'm doing this mostly for you and the others. I hain't exactly doing it for me. I don't know if I could go through with it if I was."

A shudder went through her thin body as she came out of the woods into the yard. The grass and weeds were tall. A dewberry briar caught her leg and scratched her ankle. She knew it happened but didn't feel the pain.

"It's ok," she whispered to Lacy. "It's ok. It's ok. It's ok."

She went to the front door, like a proper visitor. It was locked. She went to the back door. It was locked too. The window opened easily.

She heard his snores, loud and continuous. The sound directed her through the dark house. She entered his bedroom, stopped and looked at his bed. She watched his outline, reflected in the moonlight shining through the window. Her stomach contracted and she feared she was going to puke. She didn't. She lay Lacy down on the floor, undid buttons on the front of her dress and let it fall. She got in bed beside him, stark naked.

"What tha. . . !" He mumbled as he felt her and raised up.

"Hush," she whispered. "God sent me to you."

Chapter 17

Bobbie did puke on her way back home. She laid Lacy on the ground, dropped to her hands and knees and heaved until there was no longer bitter bile to come up. Lacy cried, the only sound Bobbie heard in the night. She forced herself to get up, take Lacy into her arms and feed her the bottle as she found her way home.

She wanted to wash herself, but she couldn't yet. She had to cook breakfast and get Clayton, Dean and Evert off to old man Clark's.

"You don't look right?" Clayton said to her as he ate.

"I didn't sleep good."

"You sick?"

"I'm tired. Just tired."

She saw Clayton look at the bed where Maw lay as he passed through the front room. Pap slept beside Maw, drunk and snoring.

How she hated the sound of snoring!

Dean and Evert lagged behind Clayton. They didn't want to work for old man Clark. They wanted to sit by the riverbank and fish.

"If you hush your bellyaching, you can take off tomorrow and Sunday," Clayton finally gave in and told them.

He had been making them work six days a week, but it wasn't hurting them none. They had gained weight and grown three inches in height. The other six boys weren't faring nearly as good. And poor little Bobbie, she was fading away right before his eyes. He wanted Maw to come back to herself. He wanted Pap to disappear off the face of the earth. Pap never done no work, except what little he helped old James Bishop at the still. He only did that to get his drinkin' liquor.

Once, Pap tried to make him work at the still in his place, but Bishop wouldn't have it. Said he wasn't having no kid working for him. Told Pap he could strain his body with a mite of work if he wanted to fill his gut with liquor. Clayton knew Pap wanted to get mean with Bishop, but Pap didn't have that kind of nerve.

Clark gave them breakfast. He always fed them as soon as they arrived and before Alva got there.

"Is it alright if these here boys take off tomorrow?" Clayton asked as he straightened his shoulders and looked Clark in the eyes. "I'll come in and work mighty hard. I'll do my bestest to make up for them two."

"If that's what you want." Clark handed them more biscuits. "There's never an end to work around here. I go to bed and wake up with it all around me. But, I feel mighty proud when I know I've done a good day's work. I know I'm a fine, capable man when I fall asleep at night."

"I know I'm a tired son-of-a-gun when I drop off at night," Evert told Clark.

"Right," Clark said. "Know what I would do different if I was your age again?"

Clayton looked at him, his blue eyes serious. "What would you do different?"

"Education," Clark said. "I'd have me a better education."

"Why, there ain't nobody anywhere with more education than you."

"Oh yes, there is. Take my wife, Mattie. She went all the way through twelve years of school, then attended four more years of college."

"Sixteen years." Clayton added quickly. "She wasted near half a lifetime and she hain't nearly as smart as you are."

Clark chuckled. "Yes she is, son. She sure enough is. One of these days I'm going to take you boys on a selling trip with me. I want you to see the world beyond our mountain hollows."

"Tell us about hit," Dean said, knowing a tale was better than going to work.

"Not right now, son. There's work out there waiting to be done, and we're men enough to do it. Makes you proud, doesn't it. Knowing we're men enough to do a good day's work."

The boys started to get up from the table but Clark motioned for them to sit and eat more if they wanted.

"I'll be just a minute. I forgot to give Mattie her new medicine. She takes it at seven sharp and it's ten after. Doctor gave her a different kind in hopes it'll help her."

Clark got up and opened a cabinet door. There had to be at least a dozen bottles of medicine in there, Clayton concluded as he watched. All that medicine given to her by a real doctor.

Chapter 18

Maw got bad sick, and Bobbie sent Frank and Grady after Sarrie Jones. Sarrie came straight away carrying a pone of cornbread and a fresh baked cherry pie. The pone was large enough to give each boy a hunk, and they each had a spoon full of pie. Sarrie noted that Bobbie let them have her share.

"You really ought to eat more," Sarrie told Bobbie firmly as she felt Maw's head and checked her heart rate. She laid her ear on Maw's chest and listened to her lungs.

"I eat plenty. I just hain't never gonna be big like Alva."

Sarrie caught her tongue before she said thank goodness for that. She lifted her head from Maw and looked at Bobbie. "She han't got fever no more. Everything seems normal. She's even putting on a little weight. Can she feed herself?"

Bobbie shook her head. "I make her eat plenty. Even when she don't want to. I spoon it in her mouth."

"Does she go to the toilet by herself?"

"I know about when she has to go. If I lead her to the toilet and sit her down, sometimes she'll do her business like normal."

"The rest of the time you change her like you do Lacy?"

Bobbie didn't answer.

"Do you put diapers on her?"

Bobbie shook her head, disgusted with such an idea. "Maw hain't no baby."

"That's a fact," Sarrie said. "And you ought not to be treating her like one. She's got to learn to do for herself otherwise she'll kill you waitin' on her."

"Will Maw be all right?"

"You mean today? I reckon she just picked up a stomach complaint." Sarrie frowned as she thought. "Has she been sitting in the grass?"

"I had her sittin' in the warm sunshine for a while this morning. She did get outta her rocker and play in the grass a while. Why?"

Sarrie nodded at the bucket beside Maw's bed. There were pieces of grass blades in Maw's puke.

"If I had my guess, I'd say she has done like a dog. She ate enough grass to make her puke."

"You don't think there's anything seriously wrong with her?"

"Law child, I think there's something wrong with her all right and it is serious. But it's beyond me to know what, and I hain't talkin' about her belly ache."

She reached out and pinched Maw hard on the arm. Maw jerked and moved her arm away.

"She's got feeling in her, and she knows to move away from pain. Why she refuses to hear what a body says to her or help herself is beyond me."

Maw was looking at the bruise on her arm. Alvin had hurt her again, but she wasn't going to think about that. She was going to sit at the spring branch and wiggle her toes in the cold water. She picked a sprig of mint growing along the damp ground and stuck it in her mouth. It made her mouth feel good, like a cool breeze entered it. She dipped water in her hand and took a little sip. Life really wasn't bad when Alvin was gone. Maybe he would stay gone for a long while this time. Maybe he just wouldn't come back at all. Maybe she could move back in with her own mommy and pa and be happy again.

"Is her female parts functioning right? Do you tear rags for her?"

Bobbie nodded and felt her face flush. "Just last week. I can't tell any change in that."

"That's good." Sarrie took a close look at Bobbie. "You hain't comin down with something are you, Child? You're lookin' mighty blue under your eyes."

"I'm just tired. There's a lot to do around here without Maw's help. I have to care for Maw and the boys all day and Lacy keeps me awake at night."

"It's a shame," Sarrie said.

"Clayton helps me a lot," Bobbie told her. "Dean and Evert help some. When the boys get a little bigger, things will be easier."

Kyle came into the front room from outside and clutched onto Bobbie's dress tail. "Moow," he begged. "Moow."

Bobbie reached down and lifted him into her arms. "All gone," Bobbie said to him. "Pie's all gone. I'll feed you something else in a little while."

Sarrie watched the little boy rub his runny nose against Bobbie's shoulder and hair. This girl had about as much of a chance at life as a piss ant caught in a sugar bowl. She'd be used up and in her grave before all these boys got big enough to do her any good. But what was there to be done? Her maw had gone crazy and her pa was nothing but a mean drunk. She had a sister that was capable of helping, but everyone knew Alva Dyke Press took care of herself. There wasn't much the neighbors could do to help. They were all, including herself, a step or two away from being as bad off as the Dykes. All it would take would be a mother or father to be rendered unable to work, and all hell would be dumped down on the children. Oh well. That was the way life was and everybody knew it.

"Bobbie Dyke," Sarrie wagged her finger as she said, "You've got a mighty hard row to hoe."

When Sarrie got home, she kissed her husband right on top of his baldhead for not being like Alvin Dyke.

Bobbie used her maw's sickness not to attend meeting for two Sundays in a row. On the second Sunday Alva showed up.

Alva looked about the place like she was inspecting a boil on the back of her hand. Bobbie wasn't keeping things up as good as Maw had, and that had been nothing to brag about. The house was dirty and what few clothes they had wasn't as clean as they could have been. The garden, the cornfield and the potato patch could use a hoeing. The yard needed sweeping and the few chickens remaining were scratching under the porch.

"Looks like you could use some help around here," Alva said none too pleasantly. "Boys," she yelled. "You get your Sunday clothes off and get your sorry asses out here. I hain't leavin' till this place is shinin' clean."

When Alva had everybody working, she dragged Maw out of bed and sat her down on the front porch.

"Maw," now you listen to me, you get over this and you get over it in a hurry or you just go ahead and die. There's no use in you killin' Bobbie, Lacy and a couple of the little boys just because you want to waller in craziness."

Maw smiled. She smelled wild roses and locust blossoms. Pa always said she was plumb crazy about those smells.

Alva turned away from her and started giving orders to get that place shaped up. She didn't even notice Pap was gone. If she had, she'd have been glad of it.

Bobbie slept after Alva left, and so did everybody else.

On Friday, three weeks to the day from the time Bobbie made her trip through the woods, Preacher Holloman showed up.

"I come to see how your maw's doin'," he said as he stood on the porch and looked at Bobbie.

She was so delicate and frail looking. Her eyes were as big and brown as a calf's. He reached out to touch her, but she took a step backward.

"I heard your maw weren't doin' so good. I know that's why you missed church the last two Sundays." He looked around to see if Alvin Dyke was about. "Alvin inside with your Maw?" He tried to enter the front room, but Bobbie wouldn't move from the doorway.

"Why don't you take yourself a seat on the porch," Bobbie suggested.

She tried to calm herself, tried to think clearly. She knew what she had to do, but she thought she would have another week or two of reprieve before doing it. She sat down in a chair close him, but not too close. He was all dressed up like he was going to preach his Sunday sermon. His hair was extra greasy and slicked back until comb marks were clearly visible. She smelled Juicy Fruit chewing gum every time he opened his mouth. He had lost weight since Ester died. She figured the neighbors weren't keeping him as well fed as he would have liked.

He looked about the place, and Bobbie was glad Alva had made the boys help clean the place up.

"Is Alvin about?" he asked again.

"No," she told him. "He hain't. He's been gone all this week."

He licked his lips, reached out his hand and placed it on her arm. She wanted to jerk away, but made herself stay still.

"Reckon we could go for a walk?"

"No," she said as softly as she could. "I don't reckon we can."

"Why not?"

"It wouldn't be right."

Disappointment creased his face. "But you come to me of your own free will."

"No I didn't. God sent me."

"Why hain't he sent you again?"

"He told me I couldn't go to you no more. He said it wasn't the right thing to do, you being a preacher and all. He said if folks ever found out, you'd be ruint for life. Nobody would ever let you preach again. You'd have to give up your house and leave here." She lifted her hand and made herself place it on his. "I could never forgive myself if I was to hurt you." She made her fingers rub his hand, slow and thoroughly.

He swallowed, looked at her and licked his lips. "God sent you to me. It'd be all right," he tried to sound persuasive. "For one more time, anyhow."

"No. No it wouldn't be. God knows it and so do I." She leaned closer as she looked up at him with sad eyes.

"God wanted me to give you a gift, but I can't give it to you no more. Why don't you go on back home and pray. God will tell you it's wrong, just like he did me."

He shook his head and twisted in the twine-bottomed chair. His need was far too great to leave.

"Bobbie, you know I'm a servant of God. *He* wants to take care of *my* needs so I will be free to serve the needs of the congregation. *He* wants that."

Bobbie gathered her courage by reminding herself what lie ahead if she hit the preacher over the noggin with a stick of stove wood. This wasn't just for her. It was for all her brothers and sisters and for Alva's kids too. It was for a tiny baby that had done nobody wrong and wasn't even birthed yet.

"Preachers need a wife," she told him. "They don't need somebody doin' an act that will bring preachers down. God meant for preachers to have wives. Preachers can't lower themselves for anything else."

She lifted her hand and caressed his face. Her thumb brushed over his damp lips then fell to her lap. Her head dropped in submissive dejection.

"I'm sorry," she whispered. "So very sorry. There's that Methodist preacher over that far hill a ways. You best find you a good woman, take her over there, and have him marry you up with her. Only a wife can give you what I gave you."

The preacher looked thoughtful.

Bobbie had carried Lacy with her while Frank and Grady looked after the younger boys. She got back after Clayton, Dean, and Evert had gotten home.

"Where you been?" Clayton demanded as he gave Preacher Holloman a hard look.

"Clayton," she said, as her eyes begged for his understanding. "You'll have to look after the boys tonight. I have to go on home with the preacher right now. That Methodist preacher just finished marrying us up a while ago."

Clayton watched her walk off following the preacher, carrying little Lacy in her arms. He tried to understand what had happened. Wanted to understand why Bobbie would marry up with a man like the preacher. He had to be nearly as old as Pap, and Bobbie never seemed to like him, so why would she marry him? He worked and worked his mind, but no answer came. What came to him was fear beyond all he had known before. As the next oldest, it was handed down for him to take care of the boys and Maw.

Chapter 19

"You hain't going back there no more," Preacher Holloman said as they walked through the woods toward his house. "You belong to me now."

"I know, but I don't reckon we'll have too much choice in the matter, at least not for a while. Folks wouldn't look on you too kindly if you married me and wouldn't let me go back to help."

"Alvin Dyke can get off his drunken ass and take care of his own family."

"Like that's gonna happen."

"He won't have no choice in the matter."

"You know I'll have to go back and help out for a while," she said. "But, I promise I won't neglect you. I married you and I intend to make you the happiest man that ever lived. That's what God told me to do and I aim to do it."

"That's what women are supposed to do," he said. "It hain't no great revelation on your part."

"Maybe not," Bobbie said softly. "But some wives might try harder than others do."

"My Ester did a fine job. A preacher couldn't of asked for a better wife."

"I know that." Bobbie thought of the bottle Lacy sucked on. Ester had given her the precious bottle she had kept all these years. Bobbie wondered what Ester would think if Ester knew she had taken her husband too. Not out of love, because there was no one else that could save disgrace from her and her kin. Somehow she didn't think Ester would mind.

Bobbie was back home before Clayton woke up. She hadn't slept much during the night.

She tried to convince herself what the preacher did with her wasn't so bad. He hadn't hurt her like Pap had done. She told herself over and over that lying next to the preacher was better than disgrace. Besides, she had a nice soft bed instead of the hard floor, and Lacy slept in a wooden cradle the preacher had pulled out of the attic. He told Bobbie he wasn't having no baby pissing in his bed.

"You're here?" Clayton asked as he saw her cooking breakfast." You still married to that preacher?"

"Yeah."

"Why did you go and do a stupid thing like marryin' him? He hain't fit fur ye."

"He hain't so bad."

"He is and you know it. Besides, Kyle cried for you most all night."

Bobbie looked at the milk gravy she was stirring. She reckoned she would have to take little Kyle with her to the preacher's house. He was still a baby, and the boys didn't know how to care for a baby. She just had to figure how to make the preacher accept him.

"Clayton, I want you to know I only married him to make things easier on us. I won't be leaving you here to look after everybody. I'll be here just like always."

"Alva wasn't the same after she got married."

Bobbie knew Clayton wasn't admitting he was glad to see Alva married and gone. Alva tried to work the rest of them twice as hard as she worked herself. Besides, Alva did all the cooking and most all the eating.

"I'm not like Alva. Now, if you and Dean could milk those two cows while I clean and feed Maw, it would be a help."

The look on Clayton's face wasn't one of conviction as he went to wake up Dean.

Bobbie sat on the side of Maw's bed thankful that Pap wasn't there. "Maw," she said as she wiped gravy from Maw's chin, and propped another pillow behind her to make feeding easier. "I'll understand if you can't come on back, but if it's in you to come back, then it's best you do it. You've left a whole houseful of younguns with nobody to raise 'em. I'm doin' the best I can, Maw, but I hain't enough. We all need you."

Maw opened her mouth and swallowed the food. It was good food, the best she had ever tasted. Her own mommy shook her head as she watched her eat.

"Ye're gobblin' that gravy like you hain't had a bit in you life. That man of yourn starvin' ye?"

How did she answer yes to a question like that? All she had to eat was what she could grub out of the woods or filch from somebody's garden. Her man was lying somewhere drunk.

"Reckon hit's because I'm in the family way," she admitted to her mommy although she thought the shame of saying it was more than she could bear up under.

Mommy turned her back and walked out the door as though a good Christian woman couldn't stomach such foul, outspoken words.

"Eat just a little more, Maw," Bobbie encouraged when Maw clamped her mouth shut. "You don't eat enough to keep a bird alive."

Maw would eat no more.

Bobbie sat the plate of biscuits and gravy on the floor. She would try to feed Maw the rest in a while. She knew Maw would never come back if she starved to death first.

"Maw, you've gotta get up and go to the toilet."

Bobbie pulled the quilt from Maw and moved her legs over the side of the bed. Maw just had to use the toilet this morning. Bobbie's stomach couldn't take cleaning her own Maw's butt like she was a baby. The thought alone was making her queasy.

Bobby struggled with Maw's weight all the way out back. Maw was in a difficult mood again and wouldn't help herself any. Finally, Bobbie got her inside the leaning, square of a toilet that sat over a small stream of water. She unpinned the diaper she had put on Maw, lifted her petticoat and sat her over the hole and waited, and waited.

When Bobbie got Maw back to the house, Clayton, Dean, and Evert were gone and the boys were awake and in the kitchen.

"My goodness!" Bobbie felt tears sting her eyes. "Get to that table like you ought to."

Slowly, the boys got up off the floor where they had the pan of gravy and biscuits and were eating like a pack of puppies. Bobbie divided out the remaining food and cleaned the floor on her hands and knees. She sniffed a time or two as she fought useless tears.

"You get back home where you belong!"

Bobbie looked up to see the preacher standing over her.

"Preacher, could you see fit to go in there and say a prayer over Maw? Ask God to make her well again."

Alva came in a hair of dropping Jay. There for a moment, she thought she saw Ester Holloman sitting in her usual place on the church pew. But, it wasn't Ester. It was her own sister. Bobbie had on Ester's Sunday dress and her head hung just like Ester's used to hang. Lacy was asleep in her lap and Kyle was snuggled up against her side. Alva sat down in her usual place and tried to hide her shock and puzzlement. She glanced across the aisle at Clayton and the boys. They were all scrubbed and pressed like Maw used to send them to church.

"What the hell's goin on here?" Alva wanted to shout at Bobbie. Instead, she let her eyes rest on Bobbie, watching, waiting. She figured she knew, and by God she had better be right for the entire congregation of Hemlock Ridge was gawking and whispering.

Preacher Holloman stood up. He was scrubbed until he shined. His clothes were starched and pressed into crisp edges. His hair had an extra dollop of hair grease. His face was that of a happy man.

"Brothers and sisters," he said. "I han't got my dearly beloved Ester back. God took her to be with him and I'll forever be in sorrow. She was the love of my life, my mate, the air I breathed. She's gone from me now and forever, but God didn't want me to be alone. He sent me Bobbie as my wife. We were married Friday evening."

Bobbie didn't move one inch or look up as the preacher talked. She rocked Lacy and tried to smile at the sleepy Kyle.

Alva watched Bobbie, the preacher, and every single person in the church house. She wished her relatives would stop being the center of attention. How could she raise herself and her children to a higher standing if her parents and siblings kept making a public show of themselves?

Mattie Clark told her yesterday people became what they pretended to be. Well, she was pretending to be a person of importance.

Now, Bobbie had gone and married up with the preacher. Alva didn't want to admit it, but Bobbie could have done worse for herself.

Alva grinned. It would be up to the preacher and his new wife to take care of all the Dykes. She sure to hell wasn't going to have them dumped on her just because Bobbie got married, unless it was Clayton. Now, she might agree to take on Clayton and in a year or two maybe Dean, the others, no sir-ree. She had Jay and she was carryin' another boy in her belly. She had her own family to look after. There wouldn't be any more of her running to help Maw. That preacher could do the running from now on.

When the meeting was over, Alva watched the crowd gather around Bobbie like a bunch of guinea hens stretching their necks to eye a curiosity. But Alva wasn't going over to her. She had spent her good time trying to protect Bobbie from that man and his lustful ways. Now, look what thanks she'd gotten from Bobbie. She balanced Jay on her hip and caught Clayton as he waited for Bobbie.

"Hay, you, Clayton. Reckon you'll be wantin' to come over and live with me, now."

Clayton looked at his sister, wide-eyed and speechless.

"Bobbie has the preacher, now. He'll take your place."

"I gotta look after Maw," Clayton finally said.

"Not any more you don't."

"You know me and Dean and Evert has to work out that cow with old man Clark. There hain't enough time in the day for me to be building on that rock house of your'n."

"I can build my own house. That hain't what I had in mind."

Clayton looked at her from head to toe. She had doubled in size since she married Pete. She'd gotten taller and broader. Her face looked to be round and soft, but there was no softness to her eyes, and her mouth held itself in a firm, straight line. Some kind of change was taking hold of her and was making her different, a worse kind of different. Clayton always wanted to stay as far away from Alva as he could get. He wanted it worse now.

"I gotta look after Maw," he told her again.

"Maw has Bobbie and now the preacher to care for her. Besides, Maw's still got Pap."

Clayton stepped backward, away from Alva. "A jug of liquor's got Pap. Allus has; allus will. Maw don't got nothin', not even herself." He hurried away from Alva and rounded up his brothers and headed home. He knew Bobbie would show up to fix them Sunday dinner as soon as she could.

Chapter 20

Alvin Dyke turned up his jug and drank until it ran out the corners of his mouth. He lowered his jug, gulped air, and drank again. The firey liquor hit his throat and traveled all the way down to his toes. The top of his head seemed to expand upward, and he was a happy man. He became a hunter with the need for game to conquer. His appetite became whetted with the anticipation as he staggered from the porch into the house. He looked for Zoe. He couldn't see her for the darkness inside the house, but he knew where she was. He staggered to the bed and gave her a shove.

She didn't move.

He opened his mouth to cuss her, but his lips had trouble with the words. He gripped her by the hair and raised her into a sitting position on the bed.

She didn't move, didn't fight, didn't make any indication that he was there or that she was alive.

He turned her loose and she fell backward onto the bed like a rag doll dropped from his hand. He slapped her across the face, then again to show her he was the man. She had to know his strength, his dominance. Teach 'em early how things stood and there would be no trouble later.

Still, she didn't respond.

His lips were moving, calling her names, but the sound was incoherent grunts. He tossed the cover from her, yanked her petticoat up over her face. He'd show her total dominance. He would show her he owned her body, mind, and soul.

It didn't work this time. He felt no victory.

"Damn freak," he mumbled as his hand wiped the moisture from his crotch. "Like fucking a corpse."

He kicked Maw out of bed onto the cold floor. She lay as she had fallen while silent tears slid from her eyes.

She saw her husband, flowing with youth, his eyes shining, his laughter full and compelling. Oh what a handsome man. He had charm that could draw the squirrels down from the tree branches. How was it a man like him had to have a body and hands that hurt?

She lay in the shade at the edge of the cornfield. Her back aching from hoeing, she thought. The need to relieve herself was demanding as she rose up and lifted her dress. She bore down causing water to gush from her. Dear Lord, this was from her baby. It was coming and she needed help. She'd never seen anything birthed before, not even a calf. Mommy had made sure of that.

"Unfittin' sight for a girl," mommy always said.

She only knew one solution. She had to find Sarrie Jones. She helped birth babies.

Clayton woke up with the morning light and climbed down from the loft to the front room. The dim light showed Maw to him. He went closer. Her petticoat was hoisted above her waist. Her private parts exposed. Clayton wanted to cry. He wanted Bobbie.

Pap was sprawled out, covering the whole bed as he snored. Clayton knew what had happened. Hatred filled him, cold and deep and complete.

He got the quilt Bobbie had used for her pallet and covered Maw's nakedness before he pulled her into the kitchen where Bobbie used to sleep. He built a fire in the cook stove and longed for Bobbie with each breath he took.

Finally, Bobbie came carrying Lacy balanced on one hip and Kyle on the other.

"What happened?"

"Pap pitched her outta bed." The look in his eyes was one Bobbie had never seen before.

"So, Pap showed up again."

"Crawled in like a snake." Clayton's mouth puckered. "And pitched Maw outta her own bed."

Bobbie handed Kile to Clayton and lay Lacy on the floor as she checked Maw. Her eyes were closed and her skin cold, but she was breathing normal. Bobbie lifted the quilt. Her petticoat was hiked up; dried fluid was on Maw's legs. Bobbie covered her quickly, knowing what Pap had done.

"She'll be fine in a while," Bobbie's voice soothed like she was talking to Lacy. "Give her time and she'll be fine in a while."

As Clayton and Dean walked toward the house from milking the cows, Clayton said, "I aim to go on in to old man Clark's. You and Evert stay here. You stay close Bobbie and Maw. If Pap acts up, one of you run for the preacher."

Dean was pleased at staying home from work then confused. "I thought you hated the preacher."

"Do as I tell ye. The preacher's a better man than Pap. Everybody is."

Inside the front room, Pap was still sleeping in bed. Bobbie toted a chair from the front porch and sat it near enough the bed for Pap to reach when he woke up. In the chair, she sat a jug full of liquor. On the floor, she sat a second jug.

🕊

"Morning, Clayton," Clark said as he answered Clayton's knock on the door.

By Clayton's timing, he was late.

"Where's your brothers this morning?"

"Bobbie needed them."

"It looks like you'll have to eat enough breakfast for them and yourself. I fixed enough for the four of us."

It was one of the few times in Clayton's life he didn't feel hungry, but he would eat. Food was hard to come by, and a man was a fool not to eat while he could.

"Clark--- Clark, can you come in here?"

"Go ahead and set down at the table, son. Mattie needs me for a minute."

Clayton sat down, but the second Clark disappeared he jumped up and opened the cabinet door where Mattie's doctor bought medicine was kept. He grabbed two of the back bottles and rushed out the door. He buried them out of sight under a rock as fast as he could manage.

"Where you been?" Clark asked when he let him in the house the second time.

"Had to take a dump. Couldn't hold it. Musta been somethin' I ate."

"Know how that is. The bathroom is the second door, yonder. Wash you hands so we can get all this breakfast eat up. Work's waiting on us."

It was the first time Clayton had ever seen an indoor toilet. He stared at it wondering if it was a clean thing to have in a house. He'd once heard Pap say, "When folks started shittin' inside the house, they'd best do their eatin' outside."

That night, before Clayton went to bed, he crammed two of the pills down Maw.

Chapter 21

Fall of the year on Hemlock Ridge came early. The first sign was the katydids hollering, then calling of the jarfly joined in with the crickets. The frogs became more intense with high pitch and deep croaking. A mountain symphony began that lasted for a few weeks and varied in tone with day or night.

When the symphony began, folks knew they had better have half their winter's canning done. They only had a short time to do the other half. A killing frost on Hemlock Ridge came in early September.

Bobbie not only heard it with her ears, she felt it in her soul. Summer time and the living is easy. Winter time and you had best been busy. She had been busy. From five o'clock in the morning until dark at night, she never stopped, never sat down. She ate her food standing up as her brain repeated the words hurry, hurry, hurry over and over. It was as though she only had a few minutes of time to take care of her world, and if she didn't, her world couldn't survive.

She had to get to Maw's, carrying Lacy and Kyle, and take care of everything there before the preacher awoke. He wanted his breakfast on the table the minute he woke up and relieved himself. He wanted biscuits and sausage gravy, runny fried eggs and some kind of fruit, usually stewed apples. Like Pap, the preacher loved milk. She was glad for the two cows. The preacher didn't have a cow.

"Mornin preacher," she greeted him in her usual manner as he took his place at the head of the table.

"Mornin'. It's cold as a witch's teat out there."

Bobbie grinned. He hadn't lingered in the outhouse this morning. She sat his food before him and let her hand touch his shoulder in the lightest of gesture. He looked up at her for this was something she never did. She took a seat in front of him. Something else she never did.

"What is it?" he asked as he shoveled food in his mouth.

"I was wonderin' if you might get the congregation to pay for your preachin services with a goat?"

His head turned and the fork of biscuit and gravy hit the side of his jaw and dropped to his plate. He stabbed it again with correct aim for his mouth.

"Goat? Why in this world would you want a confounded goat?" he asked and chewed.

Bobbie looked at the checked, plastic tablecloth. "Sarrie Jones said it was the best thing for a woman in the family way to drink. She said it would grow a strong, healthy baby."

He laid his fork down, something he never did, and stared at her downed head for a long time before he spoke.

"Just what are you tryin' to tell me, Bobbie Holloman?"

"You aim to be a daddy," she finally managed to get the words out.

"When?"

"Don't know exactly. Spring, I reckon."

She saw his thoughts working on his face. He thought of Lacy and Kyle and all the work she did for her kin. She knew he considered the work she did a good reflection on a preacher. Preachers' wives were supposed to help others, after they helped their husbands. Then, another youngun would take up more of her time. But, in all honesty, he hadn't suffered none. She gave him more time and care than Ester had given him,

God rest her righteous soul. However, this was his child. His face seemed to glow with light as the frown faded. 'God was making him a son in his very own image.' Yes, he liked that.

He'd get Bobbie a milk goat.

Bobbie looked down at her hands. They were achy but calloused. She had to can and store enough food for fourteen people. The preacher was a big eater. Pap was too, except when he was drinking. Then he was mean as a dog fed on gunpowder. The solution to Pap was to keep him passed out drunk. That way he didn't eat much, beat on Maw, or try to get hold of her.

"Preacher?" she asked again, before she got up from the chair. "I was wonderin' if you'd go over to Maw's with me? I think your prayin' helps her some. If you and enough folks prayed hard enough, Maw might get well and I wouldn't have to be over there."

Bobbie wasn't thinking any such thing. She had given up on Maw, except for a fine grain of hope. Pap was almost out of liquor. When he started to sober up, he got mean. If the preacher prayed over Maw, Pap couldn't stand it. He'd get mad and leave out. Go work at the still and earn himself more liquor to drink. The time he was gone was the best time they lived.

Pete carried home every scrap of produce old man Clark would have thrown into the compost heap.

"That bushel of tomatoes can go to the rotting pile," Clark said to Pete. "Unless Alva or Clayton want to tote it home."

Clark's rotting pile wasn't nearly as big as it was last year. Mattie was happy not to smell rotting cabbage and the like. She knew the Dykes' and the Presses' hogs were getting fat on what she didn't have to smell.

Clark knew never to offer Pete anything. He didn't want it, but Alva always did. His admiration for Alva was fading some. The determination he saw in her was turning to greed. Her needing was turning into wanting. To take stuff home before Clayton, Dean, and Evert could get it became a challenge for her. Clark made sure Clayton and his brothers worked later than Alva and Pete. That way he sent produce with them that Alva never knew about.

It bothered Clark some to know Alva had him sneaking around doing things for her brothers that he should have done openly. Alva's care for

Mattie, and her cooking, was much better when she remained happy. It wasn't a pretty sight to see a two hundred pound-plus, pregnant woman sulk up and pout.

"You treat me like I was a damned mule," Pete said to Alva as he shifted two large sacks of sweet corn on his back."

"Stop your confounded complainin'. You won't be complainin' when you're eatin' that this winter."

"What you wantin' this here corn for? Half of it's too big. It hain't like we don't have a garden of our own at home."

"You don't know nothin', Pete Press, but laziness. You outta know that everything a body has on their own just gets them by. It's what they get from somebody else that puts them ahead. Besides, that too big corn makes mighty good feed for the hogs and chickens."

"They got plenty enough to eat as it is."

"More'n enough for them to eat gives you more'n enough eggs and ham on your plate. Carry that load like a man ought to, without whinin'. I'm carryin' Jay, a boy in my belly and a full sack of corn myself."

Pete didn't tell her she ought to carry a load. She was twice the size he was. He'd never seen a woman grow as much as Alva had. She had gotten bigger and stronger. She reminded him more and more of a grizzly bear, ill tempered and independent.

"You coulda let Clayton and Dean take your sack of corn home with them. Made it easier on you."

"Humph!" Alva said. "Bobbie's got that preacher. Let him do somethin' besides run his mouth on a Sunday."

"How do you know you're carrin' a boy? Might be a girl." Pete wanted to argue with her. Prove her wrong.

"I hain't havin' no weak, simpering girls. All I'll ever raise is men. Strong men, fit for something."

Pete hushed his mouth. He didn't want to give Alva reason to tell him, again, what a no account man he was.

Chapter 22

🕊

Hemlock Ridge was like living in a bowl of ice topped with snow during the wintertime, and it was only the end of January. All but the necessities came to a stop. Pete huddled around the stove and held his hands out to the warmth as he declared the world was surely going to end, this time by freezing instead of flooding.

Little Jay Press sat on the dirt floor and played with the white snow that blew through the cracks in the log walls. He didn't seem to mind the cold as long as he was left alone to do as he wanted, when he wanted.

"You ought to go to the creek and get mud to fill those cracks." Alva told Pete as he huddled close the stove.

"Mud's froze solid." Pete reminded her. He didn't tell her she was the one that cinched the mud in the cracks the last time and ought to be doing it this time.

"Wouldn't been this cold if you'd put the roof on the rock house so we could live in there."

"You wouldn't help me do it," Pete reminded her.

"You want me to fall and kill your own son I'm carrying? How'd you raise Jay if I was dead? Reckon you'd tote him over and give him to Bobbie. She'd have her another boy she didn't have to suffer birthing pains gettin'."

"She'll be havin' them soon enough," Pete told her.

Alva turned her head and looked Pete in the eyes. "What are you sayin'?"

Pete frowned. "You didn't know your own sister was in the family way?"

"How do you know?"

"Clayton said so."

Relief touched Alva's face. "Clayton don't know what he's talkin' about. Bobbie's too scrawny to get in the family way. She's like Ester. Ester didn't have no boys by that preacher. He han't no man. He's a fat, greasy hog."

"Greasy hogs make a lot of bacon," Pete said and instantly regretted it. He knew being shut up inside the house with Alva could be comparable to being shut up in a barrel full of hungry rats. There was no way he was going to come out whole.

"You seem to know a lot about that sister of mine that a man ought not to know. If you've been foolin' with her, I'll cut your nuts out and feed them to you a pinch at a time."

"How could I fool with anybody? I han't been outta your sight since you threw me in the creek."

"You're a silent, sneakin' devil. You'd do it." She crossed the floor and picked up Jay.

Jay kicked his feet and flailed his hands as he screamed until Alva sat him down nearer the heating stove. Jay crawled right back to his skiff of snow.

"Lord, God. Is there no peace with you? Does a man have to go outside and freeze his ass off just to get away from your bitchin'?"

"Don't you foul mouth me, Pete Press."

Pete stood up, allowing Alva to have all the heat from the stove. "I'll do the feedin' early. I'll find more comfort in the barn than in here with you."

Alva almost grinned as he went out the door. She would have grinned if labor pains hadn't been trying to rip her apart. House wasn't no place for a man when a woman was fixing to give birth.

Pete cussed the rickety barn that gave little shelter from the elements. A man ought to have a decent barn to milk in. He'd have one if old man Clark paid him right. But he wouldn't get a copper out of Clark until five years was up. He worked himself to the bone and what did he get for it? Not one word of praise; not one smidgen of respect. Old man Clark paid more attention to snotty-nosed Clayton than he did to him.

He held his cold hands against the warm part of the cow's udder, in the soft space next to her body and high up the inside of her right leg, until his fingers warmed enough to milk. There wouldn't be much milk to be had. Cold kept a cow from giving milk. He was certain winter would never end. He would never feel the warm sun on his bare skin again.

Alva looked at her bed and remembered what Mattie had said about taking care of what you had. She thought of Maw's blood and birthing fluids soaking her bed all the way to the floor.

It was a fact. A body would never have nothing if they didn't take care of what they had. She wasn't ruining her bed for a few minutes comfort. Besides, what comfort could a bed give? Childbirth was pure hurtin' hell no matter where you lay.

She put two extra sticks of wood in the heatin' stove. Put a pot of water on it to boil, and built a fire in the cook stove for extra warmth and put every cook pot on the stove full of water. Steam could help warm the place. She didn't want her boy to be born into below-freezing temperature.

She got the butcher knife, whetted it on the stovetop until it was sharp, and boiled some ripped pieces of cloth to tie off the cord. Had to be really clean with that belly-cord. Germs could travel right up that cord to her boy's guts. She wasn't having nothing that was sickly.

She got a twine string and tied her dress and bibbed apron around her waist, exposing her lower body. She didn't want her dress messed up. It was too danged cold to change clothes in the winter.

She got as close to the heating stove as she dared and squatted down on the dirt floor facing a split-bottomed chair. She grabbed the chair with both hands, leaned her forehead against it, and bore down during a pushing pain with all the strength she possessed. Water gushed and began to freeze on the dirt floor. She felt the pain spread from her back to the pit of her belly. She heaved a breath of air, held it, and then bore down again. Intense pain was in her groin.

Her entire being was black with streaks of red pain. She needed relief. Had to have it. Couldn't wait any longer. She gathered herself, groaned with the intensity of her strength during her pushing. She felt bones move, her outer tissue rip. The baby came out onto the dirt floor like a plop. A moving, twisting thing of tissue was steaming in the cold air. Her hands reached down, although her head was reeling with pain, and ripped the tissue from the baby. Her fingers raked mucus from the baby's mouth as she went from her squatting position to her knees. She managed to tie the cord off twice, good and tight. Then sliced the cord between the ties with the hot butcher knife. She held him upside down, resting him against her apron covered chest, and whacked him hard, twice on his bottom with a shaky hand.

He squealed like a caught pig. She smiled with pride and self-congratulations. He was the biggest baby she had ever seen. He was fat and round and turning pink fast. She wrapped him in a clean feed sack, and then into a warm quilt. She sat down on the split-bottomed chair and slowly pulled the afterbirth out, dumping it into the slop bucket. She cleaned herself the best she could with warm water and put a folded feed sack between her legs. She lay down beside her crying baby and began massaging her uterus through the thickness of her stomach.

Little Jay had forgotten the melting snow and crawled close his mother, watching her every movement.

Pete got back to the house half-frozen and mighty glad of the heat. His eyebrows rose as he saw Alva nursing her newborn son while Jay sat on the edge of the quilt watching with interest. He gave his second son a name that would stick.

"My God," he said. "What a hoss."

Little Hoss grew fast. He was a jolly, happy baby. Good natured and slow to anger. He was the exact opposite of Jay.

Old man Clark walked all the way to Hemlock Ridge carrying a cradle he had bought especially for the high, solid sides built of wood. The sides would keep out cold gusts of winds that blew through the cracks in the Press house. He had hoped Alva could have pressured Pete into helping her finish the rock house before cold weather hit. But his hopes were fruitless.

Every bone in Pete Press's body could be described as lazy. Clark knew Pete would have considered moving from one shade tree to another a hard day's work. Doing work on a cold winter day was beyond Pete. It stretched Clark's mind to find enough inside work to keep Pete busy even when he did show up.

The cradle was filled with warm baby clothes Mattie had made along with several baby-size blankets. She had even sent several stuffed toys for the new baby and for Jay to play with.

Mattie missed having Alva help her, although Alva had increasingly gotten on the side of hard headedness and impossible to reason with. Mattie said it was just hormones. A woman had a right to be moody and uncooperative when she was pregnant and her hormones were running amuck.

Mattie told Clark to be patient with the Presses. It just took some kinds of folks longer to draw themselves up by the bootstraps than it took other folks. And there was no denying that Alva was trying a lot harder than anybody. It was that Alva had mighty big boots and mighty little straps.

"Clark?" Alva asked as soon as he set the cradle down and warmed himself a little. "How long do you reckon I'd have to work for you to earn enough to buy tin for the rock part of this house?"

"Tin's a right pricey item. You might not be able to do much work with two babies. You might better stick to tarpaper."

"Course I can work. My boys will behave themselves. Weather will break the first of March enough for me to tote 'em to your place. A body has the right to live in as decent a house as they can manage. That's what Mattie told me. Besides, I want a warm house for my boys before another winter comes along."

It would be three more years before Pete worked off the land and Clark could get rid of him. He wondered how long it would take to get rid of Alva. Then, the better part of him took over and he told himself children did need a warm house to live in. He had an idea Alva would be well on her way to a third child by this time next year.

Since Clark was close to the Dyke house, he walked on over there. He had in mind asking Clayton and the boys to come in on days that weren't fit to work. He and Mattie together might give the boys some much-needed book learning. All three boys were bright, especially Clayton.

He regretted going. He knew his sleeping and waking hours would be haunted by what he saw.

Eight boys trying to take care of one another. A woman sitting in a corner near the cook stove playing with the hem of her dirty dress. A man in bed, drunk and snoring. Clayton, trying to be the man of the house when he was just a boy. A pregnant girl carrying two babies through the snow as she tried to do more than was physically possible.

That night he prayed long and hard for God to give him the answer to helping people like these. The answer was reinforced to him, strong and final in just two words. Jobs. Education. Two more words hovered in his mind, but he wouldn't let them play dominance. Liquor, inbreeding.

Chapter 23

What seems never to have an ending, does end. Snow does melt and spring always comes to Hemlock Ridge. And the people are thankful.

Preacher Holloman preached that people are not supposed to have a life of comfort and ease. Their days are not intended to be filled with happiness. Man's lot in life is to toil and labor for his daily bread. The more people suffer here on earth, the greater their place of joy in eternity. He says life on earth is short. Eternity is a long time.

The devil gives man things of comfort and joy. He makes the pleasures of life tempting and easy to obtain. That's the way he baits them along the pathway to hell. Folks ought to know all the good things in life leads straight to hell's fire.

Bobbie closed her eyes and downed her head. She sure enough was going to spend some mighty fine times in eternity for her time on earth had shown her enough of hell. She opened her eyes and tried to remember what Alva had just said.

"You ain't gonna have that baby until late summer or maybe fall. You hain't got no more belly than a small pie punkin'."

"You might be right," Bobbie answered. She didn't tell Alva she knew the very minute her baby was started and it would be birthed long before summer.

"Alva, I do wish you'd go have a look at Maw. She ain't getting no better. She don't eat hardly nothing no more. I cram every bit of food down her"

"I've told you time and time again, I don't have enough hours in the day to look after Maw."

"I hain't askin' you to look after her. I'm doing that, me and Clayton. I'm telling you she's in a bad way. I think she might be a fixin' to give up and die."

"Fine," Alva said. "Dyin' is what she wants. Let her do it."

"She's our own Maw. You know good and well you can't go and turn your back on her."

"I'll look at her but that's all I aim to do. I hain't cleanin' that filthy place no more. I han't gonna doctor Maw and try to get her to come back to her senses. Besides, it would be the best thing in this world if she did die. The best thing for Maw, you, and the boys. If Pap got him another wife, you'd be set free."

"I hain't lookin' to be set free, but I do wish Maw would come back to herself. I don't want my own mother to die." She didn't tell Alva she was tired of hearing folks talk how birthing a baby had drove Maw crazy, how she'd turned into a drooling idiot having baby number twelve.

Alva shook her head. "You don't get what you want in this world. It's high time you learned that lesson."

Bobbie didn't tell her she sounded exactly like the preacher.

Bobbie carried Lacy and Kyle while Alva carried Jay and Rufus, whom everyone called Little Hoss. Bobbie felt a breath of warmth in the air and dreaded the next few months. She would have to do all that planting again just as soon as Clayton got the plowing done. She had to rush him up without telling him she needed to plant before her baby was born.

After Alva checked Maw, anger consumed her so totally her skin took on a funny color of blue. "I can't believe you let a thing like this happen! How could you Bobbie, even after I warned you."

Bobbie felt a little sick. She made a mistake by asking Alva to look at Maw. She would have known if she hadn't been so worried about herself and how she was going to manage everything. Now, Alva was quarreling at her like she could have stopped Pap.

"You know good and well Maw can't have another youngun." Alva slapped the flat of her palm against the wall.

"I reckon she's goin' to," was all Bobbie could get out. She didn't see why Alva was pitching such a fit. It wasn't Alva that would be taking care of Maw and another baby. It would be her caring for Kyle, Lacy, her baby and now Maw's new baby when she had it. That didn't include the other eight boys and the preacher, not to mention Pap. She wanted to cry.

"Lord only knows how far along she is. She's not as big as you are, but then Maw never did eat enough to grow a big baby. Nobody ever had a baby like my Little Hoss. Now, he's gonna be a real man."

Jay held onto the porch post and looked at Alva then at Little Hoss. He heard and understood what his momma said. He wished he could find words to tell her he was the only man she would ever need.

Instead, he sat down in the dirt of the yard, picked up a rock and threw it at Bobbie. He missed, but no one noticed him anyway.

Maw tried not to listen to her husband quarrel at her because she was in the family way for the fourth time.

He threatened to shoot her with the squirrel gun. He threatened to cut the baby out of her belly with his pocket knife. He threatened a lot of things, but all he did was hit her in the jaw with his fist and knock her down.

Bobbie tried to make Maw eat more food. She gave her several bites of food every hour she was there. She gave her sips of milk and cleaned her good every time she puked. She remembered all too well what it felt like to puke up your insides while trying to hide from watching eyes.

"Maw," Bobbie whispered. You've got to come on back. You can't go on livin' like this."

Sometimes Maw would smile, sometimes she would frown, but she never paid any attention to Bobbie. She never looked her in the eyes or felt the touch of her hand.

Clayton wouldn't be rushed on the plowing. He took time to clean out the barn and hog pens and cast the manure on the fields to be planted. Clark was teaching him well.

He told Bobbie they had to rotate their crops, and if they could grow more produce than they could use, Clark would sell it for them for cash money. He told her chicken manure was high in nitrogen, and he wanted to work extra for Clark in trade for chickens. He told her chickens and eggs went for a high price, almost as high in price as milk cows. "Folks has always got to eat," he quoted Clark. "Bobbie," he told her. "I'm right near being a man now. I think I can better us if I work everything right. Clark says there's enough of us boys to make up for Pap. Clark says liquor destroys everything that's inside a man's head, body, and soul."

"I know," Bobbie agreed. What Clark hadn't said was liquor could destroy everybody the drunk man touched. If not destroyed, it was deformed for life. "Clayton, I do wish you'd hurry the plowin'. I might not be able to plant much longer."

"You plant the taters. I'll have the garden and the corn field done this weekend." Clayton assured her. "Clark says there's a time for everything to be planted according to the moon. He said to plant taters now, and corn and beans next week. He's gonna send you some good seeds to plant. Seeds that's the new kind and hain't been crossed with no account stuff. He says seeds are like people. You need seeds that hain't no akin to each other if you want good crops."

Bobbie frowned as she listened. "Clayton, how do you get seeds that are akin to each other?"

Chapter 24

Bobbie had everything in the garden done, but the tomatoes staked when her first pains hit. She knew what it was because it was well over a week past time for her baby to be birthed. She didn't say a word to the boys. She just went to the house, picked up Lacy and Kyle and walked off through the woods.

She was doubled over and wet with sweat by the time she knocked on Sarrie's door.

"I need some help," she told Sarrie.

"Lord child, come on in here."

"No. I've got to get to the preacher's house. I've got to get Lacy and Kyle there then I can birth in peace."

"By the looks of you, you'll never make it that far."

"I will if you could carry Kyle."

Sarrie grabbed her satchel from the cupboard then picked up Kyle from the porch. Progress was slow. They had to stop every few minutes while a pain gripped Bobbie.

"Did you hurt yourself, child? Is that why this baby is comin' early?" Sarrie asked. "You hain't been married to the preacher long."

Sarrie's own words stopped her in her tracks. She turned to face Bobbie as realization hit her. "Lord God in Heaven. I wondered why you married that preacher." She spat on the ground. "If I was a man, I'd take a double bitted axe and steer Alvin Dyke."

Tears came to Bobbie's eyes.

"Does the preacher know?"

Bobbie shook her head.

"Child, you listen to me and you listen good. You fell down while you was totin' them two babies back and forth from house to house. You hurt yourself bad and I just happened to find you while I was on my way to pick branch lettuce. I helped you back to the preacher's, but pains had already hit you. Do you hear me child? Do you hear what I'm sayin'?"

Bobbie's lips trembled as she whispered, "Thank you."

"You don't need to thank me, child. You need never forget what I've told you. You tripped and fell over near that rotten chestnut log where the big rocks are."

Bobbie nodded her head and gritted her teeth.

"Where's the preacher? At home?"

"No. Gone fishin'," Bobbie said when she could talk again. "Wanted to study on his sermon."

"Humph."

To Bobbie, she sounded just like Alva.

"Child, this is the preacher's baby and don't you never let anybody say different. I'll spread the word it's a seven month baby because you were bad hurt."

"You'd lie for me?"

"It han't the first lie I've ever told. Besides, you deserve it more than most did."

"You've lied for other women?"

"My goodness, child. Life's hard enough on women without folks beatin' them down with gossip. If God had intended for women not to get in the family way before they was married, he'd a closed up their hole until they signed their name on a piece of paper."

Bobbie made it to the preacher's house with time to spare.

It was past supper time when Clayton came running to the preacher's calling for Bobbie. The preacher was sitting under a shade tree watching Lacy and Kyle play in the grass.

"Where's Bobbie?" Clayton demanded.

"In the house with Sarrie. She's birthin'. I told her not to be runnin' back and forth like she did. God warned me something bad was going to happen to her. And just like he told me, it's come about," the preacher said. "She done and fell down and started the baby coming. Sarrie said she is havin' a mighty hard time of it. What you after her for any how?"

"Maw's in a bad way."

"You'll have to go for Alva. Bobbie won't be goin' nowhere for a while. My son's takin his own good time comin' out."

Clayton wanted to go into the house to assure himself Bobbie was all right, but he knew he couldn't. Sarrie would run him off if he even tried.

Clayton waded the creek and climbed up the steep side of the hill. He ran through the woods and the pasture land, until he came to Alva's. Pete was perched on the roof nailing up green sawed lumber for rafters. Alva handed them up to him while Jay played beside the thick rock walls.

"You've got to help Maw," Clayton blurted out.

Alva leaned the board up against the rock wall. "All I've heard for the past year is, 'You've gotta help Maw.' I'm sick and tired of helping Maw when she don't want to be helped. What's wrong with Maw now?"

Clayton looked up at Pete and pretended he was talking to Bobbie. "Her time's done come I reckon."

"Hain't no way. You don't know nothing about such things."

"I know enough to know Maw's in a bad way."

"Go get Bobbie."

"I did. Preacher said she fell down and started the baby coming."

"Go get Sarrie Jones. She knows it all, according to her own opinion."

"She's with Bobbie."

"Humph!" She looked up at Pete. "You best not stop working when I leave here," She warned.

"I'll keep the boys while you're gone."

"No you won't. You get the roof on this house. I'll take 'em with me. I don't aim to be gone long."

Alva hadn't expected Maw to be birthing, but she was. She laid Little Hoss on the pallet in the kitchen and sat Jay beside him and went to Maw. She was lying in bed just like before.

Clayton left as fast as possible. "I've got to get the milking done." He told Alva.

"Humph." She ignored his leaving and examined Maw. "Hell, Maw, am I gonna spend the rest of my life pulling babies outta you?"

Maw grunted and groaned as she arched her back. Her eyes rolled around in her head then focused on Alva.

"I ought to drag you onto the floor, but I don't reckon you've got nothing worth taking care of. You're on the same stained sheet you birthed Lacy on. I see Bobbie didn't bother to make a new one. Wouldn't matter if she had."

Maw raised herself into a near sitting position as she gave a mighty push. Her moan keened to a high pitch, then went down to a deep groan.

Alva didn't have to pull this baby out of her. It was out and about half the size Lacy was. Alva cleaned it off, and her eyes bugged wide with disbelief. One of the baby's arms stopped and came to a point just below the elbow. The other arm had a hand if it could be called that. The fingers were grown together until they looked like a split calf's hoof that was made out of skin. The legs were only protrusions and the feet little nubs. Alva saw no toes. The head was too large for the body, but the face was a perfect face for a little girl. The baby wiggled and tried to suck air into her lungs.

"My God, Maw. My God in heaven! Look at this little girl you've give birth to. Hain't no way I can let her draw breath. Hain't no way she can live if she did."

A chill went over Alva's body as she looked in horror at what her hands were touching. A monster, she thought, a deformed monster to haunt her family forever, even if it never drew breath. Folks would never stop talking about what a Dyke had birthed. The news would go over Hemlock Ridge like a flash fire. The name Dyke would fall deeper underfoot than it was now, if folks knew, and they would if it lived for an hour or a day.

She knew what had to be done.

Alva held the baby up with one hand and hit it sharp in the back of the neck with the ridge of her other hand. There was a thin pop like snapping a pencil. The baby twitched a time or two before it became still. It never had a chance to cry or breathe air. Alva did what had to be done. She did it quick and efficient, but a hurt settled in her, deep and eternal.

She laid the baby, afterbirth and all on the floor. She hadn't bothered cutting the cord.

She didn't notice that Jay was standing at the foot of the bed watching everything she did.

When Clayton finished milking, Alva called him into the room and told him to put the baby into a hemp sack and bury it.

"She was born dead and deformed," Alva told him. "But don't you say nothin' to nobody, ever!"

Clayton buried the baby in soft garden dirt, said a prayer and cried.

Alva cleaned Maw up and left a rag to catch her blood. She didn't bother to rub her uterus as she covered her with a quilt.

"Go ahead and die Maw. It'd be the best thing that could happen to you now." She picked up her two boys and left the house.

Maw listened to her newborn baby cry. She reached out her hand and drew it to her full breast. She smiled as it sucked gently on the nipple. She loved her babies. Loved them with all her being. Alvin didn't. She knew Alvin wasn't much of a father, much of a man. He really wasn't worth the air he breathed. He beat on her and the children. A man that beat on those weaker than him ought to be killed.

Clayton sat on the side of the bed and spooned water in Maw's mouth. "Don't go and die on me, Maw." Tears dripped from his jaws. "Alva done

left and I don't know what to do for you. Just don't
you go and die."

He thought about the little deformed baby girl,
but he never once connected the deformation with
the pills he had been feeding to Maw.

He knew it was Pap's fault. Pap hadn't ought to
done to Maw what he did. Pap and his liquor had
all but ruined the lives of fourteen people, and Pap
had deformed a baby and caused Maw to be crazy.
It was all Pap's fault sure as God made daylight.
Clayton was sure of that.

Clayton heard footsteps cross the porch. Relief
filled him. Alva had come back to help with Maw.
But it wasn't Alva. It was Pap, drunk and huggin'
his liquor jug.

It was more than Clayton could bear up under.

"Bastard!" Blind rage filled Clayton. "You no
good drunken son-of-a-bitch." He jumped off
the bed and knocked the jug from Pap's hands. It
bounced off the wall, cracked and leaked liquor.
Clayton's thin arm shot out and hit Pap on the nose
with his fist.

Pap's eyes looked blank, confused, and then
filled with rage. He bellowed his anger as he
grabbed Clayton by the ears and rammed his head
into the wall. Clayton tried to fight as he slid down
the wall to the floor. His hands flailed at Pap in

useless little slaps. Pap's fist hit Clayton full in the face. Blood squirted from his nose and ran out his mouth.

"You little son-of-a-bitch. I'll beat the life outta you. I'll cut you up and feed you to the hogs."

° Pap got him by the hair and dragged him out the door, across the porch, and through the yard toward the chopping block.

Clayton cringed on the ground, helpless and whimpering as Pap pulled the axe free from the chopping block. He raised it high above his head, his arms strong with their intent.

The shot rang loud with an ear splitting explosion.

"Pap," Clayton whimpered as the axe dropped and Pap fell on top of it.

"A man that beats on those weaker than him ought to be killed," Maw said. The squirrel gun hung from her hand. "Drag him to the plowed ground, Clayton. Bury him deep and don't let nobody know. Where's Bobbie and the boys? Did they go fishin' after church?"

Part Three

Life Goes On

A return to
1991

Chapter 25

Mary didn't want to stop talking. The sound of her own voice countered the voices in her head. The voices talked about her, to her, and with each other.

The deputy sitting beside her was her only help in keeping the voices at bay.

"Where are you taking me? Jail?"

He fingered the cover of the paperback, tracing the outline of the contorted man. "You're going to Raleigh. Dorothea Dix hospital," he told her again.

"Why? I'm not hurt."

He hesitated as though wondering how much was safe to tell, or should be told to her. Truth was always good.

"Judge Kidd ordered you to be evaluated."

"Kid, like in a goat or child?"

"Goat."

"That's good. They don't bother goats. Lambs and children are in danger."

"Billy goat," he added.

"That's good. Nothing Biblical about a billy goat. Just that bone those men broke when they ate it. Don't know exactly where it's located in the Bible, but they was starved, and God let them kill and eat the goat so long as they didn't break any bones. That away God could bring it back to life so it could continue its purpose. That broken bone crippled it when it was brought back to life. God didn't like that, you know. He don't like things crippled up. He'd rather have them dead, I reckon. How long'll I have to stay at this hospital?"

"Couldn't say."

He looked at her hair, thin and hay textured as it stood out from her head. Her eyes darted about, looking out the windows, at passing cars, at the landscape around her. Her hands clutched and unclutched the material of her dress, which hung on her bony body. He knew if he touched her, he would feel the frailty of brittle bones, the lack of tissue to cover those bones adequately. He didn't want to touch her for there was something about her that made him uncomfortable.

"They won't put me to sleep at that hospital, will they?" Her voice was fearful. Her body tensed. "I told you before, they'll get me if I go to sleep. That's why I've still got this rotten gall bladder in me. I can't sleep."

"This hospital doesn't put you to sleep or take out gall bladders."

Relief came to her face. "If they try, I'll walk right outta there! I won't hear of it. I just won't." She looked at the driver. "I've got a right to a little happiness. Sixty years of hell is enough. I want to know what it's like to live good for a while before I die."

The deputy didn't speak and the driver was pretending she wasn't there.

"I sure do," she added empathetically. "I've drove around and looked at all them fancy houses. I even went up that mountain with Edna where they have a little house and a gate at the entrance. She cleans houses for them rich women. She was gonna get me a job doing that, but I couldn't stomach it.

"It was the way them rich women looked at me. Like I was beneath them. Like I was an animal because I didn't have their fancy talk and ways. They was sent to fancy schools to learn that talk and ways to behave. I could do it now, if I had the money. The only difference between me and them is money.

"If I had their money, I could be living like them. I bet them rich women don't have those devil worshipers chasing after them like they chase me. Money, it makes all the difference."

She leaned toward the deputy and he drew himself away from her. She noticed, but continued talking.

"They say money can't make you happy, but the lack of it can make you miserable."

An interested look came to the deputy's face. "Did your father have money?"

"Pa lived off the land. He was piss-poor. Do you know what it feels like to know folks look down on you? Do you know how it is to wish there were no eyes to look at you? Did you ever wear two different colored socks, glad to have them to warm you feet, then hear kids laughing at you for wearin' 'em?" Her eyes got bigger and glared at him. "Do you hear the crying, too?"

The deputy opened his book and pretended to read. He didn't want to listen to her anymore, didn't want to feel sorry for her. He just wanted to do his job and get her to the hospital. After he left her there, he would get him a good steak dinner. The county paid for him one meal when he made a human delivery.

When the deputy got back to Boone, he sat down in a cushioned chair and looked at Big Red. "That's the last crazy person I'm taking to a hospital. You can fire me, but I won't take another one."

"Did she give you a problem? The judge could have ordered her tranquilized before the trip," Big Red told him.

"She wouldn't stop talking. My life's difficult enough without spending four hours listening how life can be worse." The deputy's face was drawn and tired.

Big Red knew the feeling. He was drawn and tired most every day since he was elected sheriff. "Should make you appreciate what you have. Just remember life is what you make of it."

The deputy took a deep breath and let it out slowly. "Not all the time. It can be what somebody else makes out of it. Take little children. Once they've been mistreated and abused, they won't get over it, can't. It stays with them, tortures them until the day they die."

"I know what you're saying. Our job doesn't let us sleep too easy at night. Wonder why we keep doing it?"

"Hell if I know."

Some of the worst cases Big Red had investigated during the past ten years threatened to flash through his mind. He pushed them away. A man couldn't stop what people were going to do, just deal with it after it was done.

Chapter 26

Harold Mason was a genius in criminal law. He graduated from Harvard's law school top in his class. He had a good future planned for himself. He had two good offers, but they were not the ones he had his eye on. He was going to be successful, wealthy, and retire with notoriety. He had his life well planned out.

He passed through Boone on vacation and happened to see a girl walking down the street in front of Farmer's Hardware. She wore a pair of cut-off blue jeans and a pink sleeveless shirt that tied at her waist. He parked his car and followed her into Belk's Department Store. She had slender, strong muscles beneath her tanned skin, long shining hair glowing with health. Her dark eyes were sparkling with intelligence equal to any law student at Harvard. He made a complete fool of himself until she laughingly agreed to walk up the street to Boone Drug, and have a hamburger and drink with him.

They were married a year later.

The marriage proved you could take a Harvard law graduate out of the city, but you couldn't take a mountain girl out of the mountains she loved. Anna flat our refused to move up North. The mountains were her home and that was where she was going to stay. She told Harold that before she agreed to marry him, and he promised they would live anywhere she wanted if she would marry him.

Harold Mason opened his practice in Boone where he became known as the Perry Mason of the mountains, much to his cringing frustration.

Folks came to respect him if not like him. The first week his practice was open, he directed his secretary to tell all prospective clients he was booked up for the next two weeks, although he sat at his desk and twiddled his thumbs. He knew this would give an air of demand to the general public. Instead, the story leaked out and all remembered with a grin.

Judge Kidd had known Mason for ten years and respected his ability, but not some of his tactics.

Mason would do anything to win a case if it helped his reputation or padded his bank account. That was part of the reason he chose Mason to handle the indigent case of Mary Press Tate. Another part was that Kidd knew Mason's wife, Anna. He had gone to school with her, and was half struck on her himself, before Mason came along.

Mason looked at Judge Kidd as his gay eyes took on a dejected, puppy dog look. Deep furrows wrinkled above his nose. "There's no way I can take on this case. I'm up to my eyeballs with clients."

"Really? Now, you can be up to your autocratic forehead," Kidd told him with an, *'it's good enough for you'* look.

Mason respected Kidd. He was a fair Judge. He did tend to be soft hearted, but not so much as it might show to those that didn't know him well.

Mason went back to his office and slammed the folder down on his desk. He didn't need another client, one that was paid for by the state. He wouldn't even get recognition for this case. An almost free case could be a trade off if there was publicity involved. Never hurt a man to have the reputation of being *'Damned Good.'*

This was what he referred to as a NBA case. He would get Nothing But Aggravation. It would be run through the system as second-degree murder, a justifiable homicide. Kidd would slap her on the hand and give her a light sentence. End of case.

Thinking this, he looked at the folder with less aggression. He could get this over with and Kidd wouldn't assign him to another case for a while. He tapped the folder with his finger, opened it, and started to read, thinking here in the mountains, he should have gone into real estate law instead of criminal law. Mountain land was selling like there was gold underneath the rocky soil. Oh well, a real estate attorney might be more profitable but not nearly as challenging. Litigation attorneys had to be smart and able to think on their feet, he decided as he finished reading the case file.

This case had blinking lights going off in his brain, telling him to investigate deeper. It was a sixth sense he had. One he had developed over the years. Sometimes this sense made simple things complicated and complicated things simple. Sometimes he wished he could ignore it, but he seldom did.

The M'Naghten rule kept hitting him over the head like a sledge hammer. He reminded himself this was an NBA case. He wanted to get it over with as easy and fast as possible. He should plead her guilty of second degree murder, but his mind kept telling him no. He could get her off with the M'Naghten rule, innocent by reason of insanity.

Why take the easy way out when he could complicate things. Anna said those words to him often.

Selecting the jury offered no problem. Most of the prospective jurors had never heard of a place called Tamarack, much less of Jay Press. He and district attorney Avery Clawson had agreed on the jury with ease. This was a slam-dunk, cut and dried case with little publicity and no hassle, a few lines in the local paper, lost somewhere after the front page. No big deal.

As long as he didn't bring up the M'Naghten rule, things would ride on by without a ruffle. And, he didn't want to go into this case that deep when there was no reason.

A lot of people lived on Hemlock Ridge and Tamarack. The Press family had a profusion of relatives. And a whole lot of people had seen Jay press's picture with a beard of bees, and bought honey from the man. He had become an icon of curiosity. One that people remembered.

A crowd showed up on the day of the trial.

People filled the courtroom, leaned against the walls and stood in the halls discussing the event. A roar hummed throughout the building like the vibrations in a beehive.

Judge Kidd called Mason and Clawson into his chambers.

"I'm going to delay this case for two hours." Kidd told them. "In order for the crowd to thin. I don't want a dog and pony show."

"Does the case need to be postponed?" Clawson asked.

"The woman is over sixty years old, and is now determined competent to stand trial. I see no reason for a postponement. Just a short delay for spectators to thin down."

Kidd's words both excited and depressed Mason. Excited him in the challenge of having a trial by jury, the public, and the media. Depressed him in his lack of preparation time to give this many people the opportunity to see him at his dazzling best. He grabbed the nearest phone, after he left Kidd's chambers, and called his assistants. Kidd might not want a dog and pony show, but the crowd did.

Mary Tate felt herself trembling like she had

palsy as she entered the courtroom and took her seat beside Mason. In the past hour and a half, he had her gone over like a prospective Miss America contestant in reverse.

Her hair had been undone. Her face scrubbed of makeup. A new dress, two sizes too big, was brought for her to wear. Her vanity made her want to look good, but she knew she didn't. She looked like a drab old woman, like anybody's grandmother, one that was near drying up. Mason made her look this way, intentionally.

Mason gave her a quick smile and patted her on the arm. It didn't do her much good, didn't ease her nerves.

"All rise for the court."

All stood. Mason lent Mary a hand, although she didn't need it. She was still capable of standing.

Kidd entered in his black robe. Mary sucked in a breath loud enough for the jurors to hear. Her eyes got big, and Mason placed his hand on her back in a calming motion. He hadn't expected this reaction from her, but he was pleased with it. It wasn't faked and he planned to find out what caused it.

Kidd's black robe folded itself around him as he seated himself behind the bench.

"All be seated."

Mason helped Mary's rigid body down into the chair.

"Good morning ladies and gentlemen of the jury. I trust you are all well this morning and ready to perform your duty as jurors." Kidd's eyes studied each juror, accessing their ability to be just and accurate. He wasn't one hundred percent pleased with the jury selection, but then he never was.

They all nodded their heads.

"I must ask you not to discuss this trial with anyone, including each other. Not to listen to television, radio, or read any kind of newsprint concerning this case."

Mason wasn't listening to Kidd. His attention focused on Mary. She stared at Kidd as though the devil himself was sitting before her.

"What are you afraid of?" Mason wrote on his note pad and placed it in front of Mary.

Her eyes reluctantly left Kidd to read the question. He handed her his pen.

"Is he a devil worshiper?" She scrawled in shaky letters.

He took the pen from her. "No!" He wrote, very pleased.

Kidd was talking, looking at the crowd filling the courtroom. "I require total silence in my courtroom. No talking, whispering or milling about. If anyone conducts themselves in a manner I do not approve, I will have them removed and not allowed to reenter the courtroom. Is that understood?"

The drop of a pin could be heard.

"The trial is now ready to begin. The attorneys will make their opening statements. I caution the jury that nothing the attorneys say in their opening statements is testimony and not to be taken as evidence. Mr. Clawson, do you wish to make your opening statement?"

Clawson got up slow and deliberate as he moved his body in front of Mary and Mason. He had planned to hesitate before Mary, hoped she would be looking down as though guilt ridden. Instead, she was staring at Judge Kidd like he was Godzilla come to life. He moved on and stopped before the jury.

"Ladies and gentlemen of the jury, this is a simple case. Mary Press Tate admits to killing her eighty-year-old father. I shall prove beyond a reasonable doubt she killed him willfully and knowingly..." he continued, enjoying the eyes watching him, the silence in the courtroom as his voice grew in authority. He gave pretty much the same spiel as he gave in all murder cases. Told how it was the jury's duty to punish a murderer, how it was written in the Bible *Thou shalt not kill*. Murder in the eyes of God and the law of mankind would and should be punished. An eye for an eye and a tooth for a tooth.

After twenty long, drawn out minutes, he ended by saying, as he pointed his finger at Mary, "This woman, the daughter of an eighty-year-old decrepit man, in premeditated, planned out, and coldblood, murdered her own father."

Clawson finished with an accusing finger still pointing at Mary as he took his seat.

Mason stood up. Mary panicked, grabbed hold of the tail of his suit coat.

"Please, don't leave me," she whispered, but it was loud enough for the jury to hear.

Mason pried her fingers from his coat and held her cold fingers in his hand. He didn't stand before the jury. The jury had to look at him standing there, holding Mary's hand.

Judge Kidd was frowning ever so slightly.

"Ladies and gentlemen of the jury. Mr. Clawson has presented you a mighty fine speech on how a criminal should be punished. I agree whole-heartedly that all criminals should receive just punishment for their crimes. This case is no exception. I want the perpetrator of this crime punished. Unfortunately, it is many years too late for that to happen.

"Jay Press is already dead and buried in a Christian cemetery along with Godly people. That may be a greater crime than we have here today.

"By the time this trial ends, you will know without any doubt whatsoever that Mary Press Tate is the victim not the criminal."

He finished, leaving the jury to sum up his and Clawson's different styles of presentation. Clawson talked a lot to say a little whereas he talked a little to say a lot. So Mason thought.

"Mr. Clawson," Judge Kidd said. "You may call your first witness."

"The state calls Doctor Bryan Koller."

Dr. Koller took the stand, placed his right hand on the Bible, and swore in.

"Doctor Koller will you state your full name please."

"Bryan T. Koller, Doctor of Psychiatrics at the Dorothea Dix Hospital in Raleigh."

"Doctor Koller, tell me, what was your relationship to Mary Press Tate?"

"I was her physician at Dorothea Dix."

"As her physician, what is your conclusion to her mental state?"

"She has a psychosis brought on by stress."

"In your professional opinion, is Mrs. Tate

legally insane?"

"No." Doctor Koller answered firmly. "It is my opinion that Mrs. Tate is sane and legally competent to stand trial."

Clawson finished his questioning and took his seat with a satisfied expression.

Mason leaned over and whispered to Mary. "You have to sit here while I crossexamine him."

Mary frowned, and turned her face away from Judge Kidd and made a cross in the air with her finger.

"It's all right. You have nothing to be afraid of," Mason told her just loud enough for the jury to hear.

Mary focused on Mason, obviously not looking at Judge Kidd.

"Doctor Koller, do you know the legal definition of insanity?"

"Yes."

"Would you state it please?"

"It is a psychosis in absence of correct assessment of reality."

Mason nodded as though he were deep in thought. "Can you tell us what might cause such a psychosis?"

"Certainly. There are several contributing factors. Genetics is a strong factor. Uncontrolled stress can be another, both mental and physical stress."

"Did Mrs. Tate have any physical problems to your knowledge when she entered Dorothea Dix hospital?"

"Yes. She was in urgent need of gall bladder surgery, and she had a lung collapse."

"Why did her lung collapse?"

"I am not qualified to answer that. You will have to check with a specialist in that area."

"Are you qualified to comment on why she never had gall bladder surgery?"

"Yes."

"Would you care to tell us why?"

"At the time she had an unreasonable fear of Satanist or Devil worshipers as she called them. She believed there was a group of them in Watauga County and she was certain one of them would kill her if she slept."

"Does she still have her gall bladder?"

"No."

"Why not?"

"It was removed, of course."

"Oh, I see. Mrs. Tate got cured of her fear psychosis long enough for her to agree to have surgery?"

"I didn't say that."

"Did she get over her fear of being put to sleep?"

"No."

"She was put to sleep against her will?"

Doctor Koller nodded his head. "It was necessary in order to save her life."

"Doctor Koller, you stated that Mrs. Tate had a fear of Devil worshipers killing her if she was put to sleep. Is that not an absence of correct assessment of reality?"

Doctor Koller considered for a few moments. " It is highly likely."

"Mrs. Tate had a bad gall bladder to the extent surgery was forced upon her, also a collapsed lung. Is that considered physical stress?"

"Yes. I would term it that."

"Did you know that Mrs. Tate had been separated from her husband?"

"Yes. That was brought out in my initial examination of her."

"What about her family history? In my records, it states that Jay Press had been committed to Broughton Mental Hospital twice. Did you know that?"

"Yes."

"Did you know that her grandfather, Pete Press

had been treated on several occasions for mental problems?"

"Yes."

"Did you also know that Mrs. Tate had been treated for mental problems in the past?"

"Yes, I'm fully aware of that."

Mason turned from Doctor Koller and faced the jury. "Now let me get this straight. You said the legal definition of insanity is absence of correct assessment of reality. Number one: Mrs. Tate had a fear of being put to sleep because of Devil worshipers. She was also sleep deprived because of her fear. Two: She was under physical stress due to her gall bladder and a collapsed lung. Three: She was under mental stress from separation to her husband. Four: Her father, as I have here in my records, and several other family members, including her grandfather, have a history of mental problems. In addition, five: Mrs. Tate herself has a history of mental problems and has sought help from several different organizations and hospitals." He turned from the jury to face Doctor Koller. "Just how can you state that Mrs. Tate is not legally insane when she meets every criteria you have stated?" Mason did not give him time to answer. "Your honor, I have no more questions for the learned doctor." He turned and walked back to his seat beside Mary.

"Mr. Clawson, would you like to redirect your questioning?"

"Yes, your honor." He crossed the floor and leaned his arm on the stand in front of Doctor Koller. "In your professional opinion, is Mrs. Mary Press Tate legally insane?"

"No," he said calmly and with assurance.

"No, even though she has all the symptoms?"

"Because a person exhibits all the symptoms of a disease, does not mean they have the disease."

Chapter 27

Clawson called deputy Michel Aaron to the witness stand and stood before him in silence for several minutes.

"Would you please state your full name and profession?"

"Michel L. Aaron. I am a deputy for the county of Watauga."

"My records state you were the first to arrive at the scene of the murder, is that correct?"

"Along with the Sheriff and one other deputy."

"You are the one that kept all the notes?"

"Yes, sir."

"What did you find at the crime scene?"

Aaron looked puzzled. "Find? Like what?"

"That's what I'm asking you, Deputy Aaron. What did you find?"

Aaron shrugged his shoulders. "The most obvious was a dead man, Jay Press and the defendant Mary Press Tate."

"Jay Press was dead? Why?"

"Yes. He'd been shot."

"By whom?"

Mason considered objecting. It was not proven at this point, that Mary had been the one that shot and killed him.

"His daughter, Mary Press Tate."

Clawson turned toward the jury and pointed toward Mary for an instant. "Did she admit to killing her own father?"

"Yes."

"Yes." Clawson repeated louder for the jury's benefit. He made a display of going to his table and picking up a notebook, and returning to stand before Aaron.

"I have in my hands the notes you took that tragic day. I'm going to read Mrs. Tate's own words and I want you to tell me, to the best of you memory, if they are correct."

Aaron nodded.

"Sheriff:-- What's your name?"

"Mrs. Tate:-- Mary."

"Sheriff:-- Mary What?"

"Mrs. Tate:-- Tate."

"Sheriff:-- Mary Tate. Who's he?"

"Mrs. Tate:-- Pa."

"Sheriff: --What's his name?"

"Mrs. Tate:-- Jay Press."

"Sheriff:-- You're Mary Press Tate? You make a note here that she nodded her head, yes."

"Sheriff:-- Who shot him?"

"Mrs. Tate:-- Me."

"Sheriff:-- You shot your father? Here again she nodded her head to answer yes. Do you remember taking this statement?"

"Yes."

"Deputy, did you find the weapon that killed Jay Press?"

"Yes."

"Where did you find it?"

"Lying on the ground."

"Did Jay Press also have a weapon?"

"No, sir."

"So, Mrs. Tate killed her father in cold blood?"

"I object, your honor. Mr. Clawson is neither making his opening or closing statement here," Mason said in a bored manner as though Clawson's statement was hardly worth the effort to object.

"Sustained," Kidd said.

Clawson continued his questioning on the same line, making sure the jury had firmly established in their mind that Mary Press Tate had shot and killed her father with her own weapon while he had none.

When it was Mason's turn, he put on no theatrics. He walked straight to deputy Aaron.

"What was Mary Tate doing when you arrived on the scene?"

"Nothing, actually. She was just sitting on the ground holding her father's head in her lap."

"Holding her father's head in her lap?"

"Yes, sir."

"Was Mary crying?"

"Not so much at the time. She'd cried herself out and was just kind of hiccupping."

"In your own words, Deputy Aaron, tell us why Mary said she shot her father."

"Well, she said he threatened to cut her up with the axe and feed her to the dogs."

"Did you see an axe?"

"Yes."

"Did you see dogs?"

"Yes."

"Did the dogs look hungry?"

"I object!" Clawson said with irritation. "How would he know if a dog was hungry?"

"Sustained."

"Let me put this another way, deputy Aaron. Were the dogs fat or skinny?"

"Real skinny with their ribs showing."

"Did you see any evidence that Jay Press had attacked his daughter in any manner?"

"Yes, sir. Her neck was bruised where he choked her. She had scratches on her neck and the lab tests showed her skin under his finger nails."

"Deputy Aaron, when one person shoots another person that is choking them, is it usually considered self-defense?"

"Yes, it is."

"I object," Clawson said.

"Overruled," Kidd returned.

"You find it reasonable that Jay Press told his daughter he was going to cut her up and feed her to the dogs, and then when he proceeded to choke her, Mary believed her life was in grave danger?"

"I object."

"Your honor, Mr. Clawson opened up this line of questioning when he read a portion of Mary's statement. I think it is in order for me to continue it."

"Overruled. Continue."

He turned from Judge Kidd to Deputy Aaron. "Did you believe Mary thought her life was in danger?"

"Her life was in danger. He was three times her size."

"Thank you, Deputy Aaron. Can you tell me to the best of your knowledge, did Mary realize her father was dead?"

"Well, she said he wasn't dead."

"What were her actual words, to the best of your memory?"

"She said she was watching him because he wasn't dead. She said the bees would sting him because he had blood in his beard. The sheriff told her he was dead and she said, he ain't dead. You can't kill poison ivy."

"Did she say anything else that didn't make good sense to you?"

"There wasn't much she said that did make sense."

"Such as?"

"Well, she thought we were going to put her in a hay baler. She said she didn't want to be run through one. She said she was in pain and kept hearing babies crying in her head. She told me the crying in her ears was like a ringing in other people's ears."

"I object your honor. I read no such thing in Deputy Aaron's notes." Clawson stood up.

"When did she tell you about the ringing in other people's ears?" Judge Kidd asked.

"When I drove her to Dorothea Dix Hospital."

"Overruled. Continue."

Clawson sat back down, his movements screaming irritation.

"Did Mary ever mention Devil worshipers to you?"

"All the way to Raleigh. She was scared to death of them. She said they harmed children and baby lambs."

Mason nodded and looked at Mary sitting hunched up with her head hanging.

"Deputy Aaron, in your line of work do you come in contact with people you think are legally insane?"

"Oh, yes. Often."

"Is Mary Tate one of these people?"

"Without a doubt."

District Attorney Clawson objected.

When Mason finished with his questions and took his seat, Mary turned to him and whispered in a voice loud enough for most everyone to hear.

"You're trying to say I'm crazy. Well, I'm not. And don't you be telling folks I am. It hain't so."

Judge Kidd banged his gavel. "Silence in the courtroom," he demanded. "We will adjourn until 2:00 PM.

Chapter 28

Rufus Press got up from his seat, and just kept rising upward. Although he was seventy-nine years of age, he was still a big man. His eyes looked around the room, alert, attentive. His face was lined with age and his large head was covered in thick, white hair. He was slightly bent, like his wide shoulders were a little too heavy for his back to carry.

The jurors watched Rufus walk to the witness stand and take a seat. Mason hoped, if they associated his size to Jay Press, they would know Mary was no match for the likes of him.

Rufus looked toward Mary after he was sworn in and smiled.

Mason took his time approaching the witness stand. He wanted every juror to be looking at the big man, associating him with his brother Jay.

"You are Rufus Press, the second son of Pete and Alva Press?"

"Yeah. That's right." His voice had a slight tremor caused by age.

"Jay Press was their first born child?"

"Yeah. That's right, too."

"How many children were there total, born to Pete and Alva?"

"Well, let's see now. There were eight boys and one girl. Maw said she never wanted any girls. She quit havin' babies after she had Lulu. She said God had finally turned against her."

"Why?"

Rufus looked at him hard. "She didn't want no more girls, that's why."

"Why did she think God had turned against her?"

"Well," Rufus looked a bit bewildered. "I reckon it was because she had made a pack with God. She would stop havin' younguns when she had one that was a girl."

"Why would your mother make a pack like that with God?"

Clawson started to object, but Kidd motioned him to be silent.

"I reckon I know that one, too. Most folks said she hated girl babies, but that weren't true in my opinion. To my way of thinkin', she knew what hardship it was to be a girl child. Women had it rough back in them days. No paintin' up their faces and runnin' around pert nigh necked like they do now."

"Are either of your parents alive?"

"Naw. Maw lived to be the oldest. She was eighty-two when she died around fifteen, sixteen years back."

"How about your father?"

"Now, let me see. I reckon he was around my age when he passed on."

"Where was he when he died?"

"He was still down there in Morganton."

"By Morganton, you mean Broughton the mental hospital?"

"Yeah."

"How long was he in Broughton?"

"Well, now, I'd have to set down and figure that one up. He was there off an on ever since I was near grown."

"Were there any others in your family that were in Broughton?"

"None of my kids are, if that's what you're askin'."

"What about your mother or your brothers or sister?"

"Only Jay, a time or two. Some of the rest of us might have needed it but we didn't get sent there."

A slight snigger traveled through the crowd. Judge Kidd banged his gavel once, sharply. All was silent.

"Are all your brothers and sister healthy?"

"The ones that are alive are reasonably so."

"Do they have anything that ails them?"

"Doctor said Mac was an ect-leptic, and John has sugar in his blood. Sister Lulu ain't never done much, but I don't reckon that's because she has anything wrong with her."

"By ect-leptic, do you mean epilepsy?"

"That's what I just told you."

"Were you close to your brother?"

"Which one?"

"Jay."

"Well, now. I wouldn't go so far as to say we was close. I knowd him since I was born, but we was never close, like."

"Would you say there was a reason for not being close?"

Rufus looked at Mason long and hard. "Reckon folks can always find a reason for things."

"What would your reason be for a lack of closeness between you and Jay?"

"He had quare ways and I didn't."

"Can you describe his quare ways?"

Rufus thought about it for a while and shook his head before he spoke. "I reckon a quare person don't do things like us normal folks."

"What did Jay do that wasn't normal?"

Rufus grinned. "Don't reckon I'll live long enough to tell you all that."

Mason smiled. "Did he have quare, or odd ways sexually?"

Rufus puffed up and gave Mason a hard look. "Sir, there's women present here, and I don't reckon it's fittin for you to be talkin about such things in front of them."

The crowd laughed and Judge Kidd banged his gavel and ordered silence.

"One more outburst in my courtroom and I'll have the room cleared. Mr. Press, we do understand and agree that sex is not tastefully discussed in mixed company, but this is a court of law. Unfortunately, such topics as sex must be discussed at times. Please answer whatever questions you are asked and try not to be offended by them." Judge Kidd told him.

Rufus Press nodded. The expression on his face stated his dislike of the order.

"Did Jay Press have odd ways sexually?" Mason repeated.

"You ought to know that's so, or we wouldn't be here now, would we."

Clawson twisted in his seat. Judge Kidd gave him a silencing look.

"Could you go into a little more detail?"

"No, I can't."

Mason leaned against the witness stand and looked Rufus Press in the eyes. "Mr. Press it is very important to know this. Did Jay Press have inappropriate sexual relations with either of his daughters?"

"I never was a witness to such a thing, but I heard it was so. I never knew he was plumb insane about sex until all this came out."

When it was Clawson's turn, he stood between Rufus and the jury. "Do you have a nick-name, Mr. Press?

"Folks call me Little Hoss."

"Why is that?"

"I'm right big, big as a hoss." His face showed he was pleased with his size.

"Was Jay Press as big as you?"

"Nobody's as big as me. Jay was big, though." Rufus added before Clawson could stop him. "Big and mean."

"Did you know Mary Press Tate when she was a child?" Clawson asked.

"Of course."

"Was she quare, too?"

"No. She weren't exactly quare, just tough. Had to be with that sassy mouth of her'n."

"Did Mary sass her father?"

"Mary sassed everybody. It was just her way."

"You are telling us that Mary was a sassy child that defied her father?"

"It's a fact that Mary had a sassy mouth on her and she had sassy ways, but there's nobody that ever defied Jay." Rufus shook his head. "Reckon that's why Jay whipped on her so much. She's too much like him."

"Were you close to her?"

Rufus moved about a little. His face grew flushed and he seemed to puff up in size. "You hain't askin' me if I'm sexually crazy like Jay, are you?"

"No, sir." Clawson added quickly as the crowd stifled their snickering.

"You best not be. I hain't a man to be put down like that, especially by a smart elick lawyer."

Judge Kidd lifted his gavel and opened his mouth. He lay the gavel down silently.

"No more questions, your honor," Clawson said.

Chapter 29

Mason called Lulu Press Watson to the witness stand.

"You are the youngest child of Pete and Alva Press? Mason asked of her.

"Yes."

Her cheeks were rosy and her body rounded. Her eyes had a gentleness to them as she looked at Mason. She wasn't exactly smiling, but the expression on her face gave the appearance of a smile.

"Mrs. Watson, can you tell us in your own words about your mother?"

Her face looked a little blank, but the smiling expression was still there.

"She was a tough woman. There wasn't much she couldn't do."

"What about your father? What kind of man was he?"

"Well, I reckon you can say he was gentle.

He didn't like any kind of fuss or fighting. He'd hide from it if he could."

"Did your mother, Alva Press, like to fuss and fight?"

"I wouldn't go so far as to say she liked it, but she never turned away from it neither."

"Were you afraid of your mother?"

"Good Lord in Heaven, yes. Anybody with any sense at all was afraid of her."

"Was she abusive?"

"I wouldn't say she was abusive."

"Did she ever whip you or the boys?"

"She certainly did. I've had the blood cut out of my legs with a keen hickory switch more times than I can count."

"Can you explain what you did to deserve such punishment?"

"Just being a child, I reckon. You know how rowdy children are. Always getting into stuff and the like."

"Did she whip the boys with a hickory switch?"

"No. A switch wouldn't have affected them much. She took a belt to them."

"Did she whip Jay?"

"Most every day of his life."

"Why?"

"He was the hard headed one. Always under her feet, in her way. He wouldn't do a thing she said, but wouldn't stay away from her either."

"Why's that?"

"Because he was her first-born, I reckon. He wanted to be her man, the most important person in her life."

"He wasn't?"

"Oh no. She was the only important person in her life."

Mason rubbed his hand through his hair. "Mrs. Watson, did you like your mother?"

She was silent for a minute. "I loved and respected her, but I can't bring myself to say I liked the person she was."

"Could you tell us what kind of person she was?"

Lulu Watson frowned and appeared to be in deep thought. "Mercy, how would a body begin to describe her? Physically, she was big, almost as big as Little Hoss. I've seen her hit the old mule over the head with her fist so hard it staggered him. I've seen her pick up and tote a rock none of the boys could even roll."

"Did she like people?"

"No. I don't think she did. I can't say I ever heard her say a kind word about anybody."

"Did she ever have a friend?"

"Oh, no. Never."

"Did she like her sisters? There were two of them weren't there?"

"Bobbie and Lacy. She never spoke too highly of Bobbie. Thought she was soft and weak. Thought she had an easy life being married to a preacher and only having one child. I think she pretended Lacy didn't exist." She frowned. "As for Grand Maw, her own mother. I can rightly say she hated that woman until the day she died. Didn't even go to her funeral. I asked her why she wouldn't go to her own mother's funeral and she smacked me in the mouth. That was the last time I ever questioned her on anything."

"Mrs. Watson, I've heard there is a story on how you got your name. Would you please tell us?"

"Well, like Little Hoss said, Maw never wanted a girl baby. They said she swore she would have all boys. When I was born, she took one look at me and said 'now, this one's a lulu.' The name stuck."

Mason walked in front of the jury, then back to Lulu. He wanted her words to sink in.

"What about your grandfather, Alvin Dyke. What did your mother think about him?"

"That I can't answer. He run away long before I was ever born. Nobody ever heard of him again."

"Your mother never mentioned him?"

"No."

"Not even once?"

"Nothing that I can recall. I knew he was a bad drunk, and I knew he would take spells of being gone for weeks at a time. One of those times he never came back. That's all I know."

Mason just nodded his head. "Did you like your brother Jay?"

"He was about grown when I come along."

"Did you like him?"

She shook her head. "No," she said.

"Why not?"

"Just like Little Hoss said, he was quare."

Mason paced in front of her. Stopped, looked her in the eyes. "Mrs. Watson, I know this is going to be a difficult question for you. I know you won't want to answer it, but you are under oath to tell the truth. You will have to give a truthful answer. Do you understand?"

Her eyes were wide. Her round cheeks trembled. She looked away from Mason, down to her hands in her lap.

"Lulu, did your brother, Jay Press ever sexually abuse you?"

She closed her eyes, let her chin drop to her chest and gave a slight nod of her head.

"I'm sorry, Mrs. Watson, but you must answer that question out loud."

"Yes," she said. "Oh, God, yes."

Mason was silent for a full two minutes as he turned each page in a small notebook he carried. "No more questions, your honor."

"Mr. Clawson, do you wish to cross-examine this witness?" Judge Kidd asked.

Clawson shook his head as he looked at the note pad lying on the table in front of him.

"No questions, your honor."

"You may step down, Mrs. Watson." Judge Kidd told her.

She didn't move, didn't appear to hear his words as drops of tears dripped off her chin and landed on her massive breast.

"Mrs. Watson, you may step down."

"No. Not till I've had my say. You can't blame Mary for killing him. I've wanted to do that same thing since I had mind enough to know what he was doing to me. Mary done good. It was a good killin'."

"Help her down." Judge Kidd ordered a deputy. "Strike her words from the record. Jurors you are to disregard what Mrs. Watson just said."

Mason took his time standing up. "Your honor. I respectfully disagree. The jury has a right to know what kind of man Jay Press was."

Judge Kidd turned cold eyes on Mason. "Sit down Mr. Mason. If you question my decision again, respectfully, or not, I will have you on contempt charges. Is that clear?"

"Yes, your honor."

Mason sat down. He was pleased with Mrs. Watson, himself and Judge Kidd. The jurors would not forget.

Chapter 30

Mason knew he needed her. She was a key that would fit the lock he needed opened. Yet, he was hesitant to put her on the stand.

She rose from the crowd like a small drone bee rising from a swarm. She was dressed in dung brown, from her shoes to the thin ribbon tying her long gray hair at the nape of her neck. She showed signs of once being tall. Now, she was bent over with her back humped and her bony shoulders rounded forward. Her skin was weathered brown and worn thin and wrinkled. She looked as though something had sucked all the fluid from her body a long time past. Her little blue eyes peeked out beside a long beaked nose, a Clorox bleach faded blue for her eyes.

Mason wondered if she would get lost before she made her way to the witness stand. People kept pointing her in the right direction. Was this a witness he wanted? Was he making a mistake with her? Maybe, but he needed her just the same.

"Do you swear to tell the truth and nothing but the truth, so help you God?"

"Yes, sir. I allus tell the truth. I don't like to swear on the Bible, though. God might not take too kindly to that. You best not take too many chances with God here on this earth if you wanna keep him on your side."

"Good day, Mrs. Press. I hope you are feeling well." Mason said to stop her muttering.

"Good as abody could expect. Don't pay to expect too much here on this earth."

"Mrs. Press, can you state your full name, please?"

"I'm Ivy Fern Press."

"You were married to Jay Press?"

"Reckon I still am, if he was alive, which he hain't."

"When did you leave Jay Press?"

"I left him pert near every day of my life. I just come back when night-time come on. I's allus been afeard of the dark."

"When did you leave him for good and did not go back. Do you remember what year it was?"

"I remembers it a sight. That was the time he stuck my head in a bee gum full of them bees. He figured they couldn't blame him if them bees stung me to death. He wanted me dead."

"What year?"

"It was 1955. Them two no account doctors claimed I was a lyin'. Never did hold no faith in them two ever again. Some folks don't know what they's talkin about even when they've had a pile of edge-e-cation and claim themselves to be doctors."

"What did they claim you lied about?"

"My girls. They said Jay wasn't abusing 'em when he was. Started it when they was babies, he did. He's a mean man, I tell you, a mean man. I can't put into words what he did to me and my girls."

Her head was jerking from side to side in a nervous twitch. Her hands gripped each other as she tried to keep them from trembling.

"He deserved a killin, he did. Had I a mite of backbone, I'd a done it. Regretted it many a time that I didn't find a way to do it. Shoulda got his squirrel gun and shot him dead between the eyes while he slept. Look what it's come to now cause I didn't."

Mason glanced at the jury. Each one had their eyes glued to Ivy Press.

"What has it come to?"

"Well, just looky yonder at my first born. Settin there in that chair like she was a common criminal. Never figured she'd outlive him. He focused mainly on her, wouldn't leave her be. I figured he'd kill her afore she ever got good and growed."

Mason gave Clawson and Judge Kidd a quick glance as Ivy talked. They were both hanging their heads, intent on their hands. Neither was offering to give any objections so he continued.

"What did he do to her?"

"Oh my, what didn't he do? He'd drag her into the wood shed, barn, or woods. Once he had her in the cold creek. I thought he'd finished her off for certain that time. Poor little thing. She weren't nothin but a helpless girl baby. They were all four babies, little innocent babies." She lifted her hand up into the air like they were claws. "God knows I done all in my power. I told folks what he was up to. Told the sheriff and them doctors. Nobody listened. Not one." She shook her head and half of her thin hair fell loose from the brown ribbon. "Twicest. Once in 1953, again in 1955 they listened to me for a spell. Brought him up before the judge. Thought something aimed to be done that time, but them two lyin' doctors lied for him. Look what their lyin' did to my girl. They sent her away to that refarm school place."

Mason interrupted her. "Mrs. Press, according to the information I have, the court sent Mary Press away to a reform school for girls because she had falsely accused her father of having sexual intercourse with her."

"He told her he'd kill her if she told 'em the truth. He'd a done hit too. He made her tell 'em she was a lyin'. She was afeard just like I was. Why, he aimed to kill me and I knowd it. I had to run off with my head all swelled up and leave my four girls behind. Not abody would listen. Not abody." She shook her head in the saddest of motion. "Have ye ever noticed how men believe other men? Don't want to listen to a woman or youngun. Men, they'll stick together like two slabs of hog fat."

"Mrs. Press, was there not one person that could testify to what Jay Press was doing to his children? Couldn't Mrs. Watson have testified in your behalf?"

"There warn't nary a soul. Poor Lulu was afeard for her own life just as I was. Why, everybody what knew Jay Press was afeard of him. He'd a kilt 'em in a blink of an eye. Only wished he'd a died the day he was birthed. He's the cause of me knowin' about them Devil worshipers." Her eyes took on a glazed-over look. "One night I hunted through the woods till I come up on 'em, and me skert of the dark like I was. I aimed to have 'em torment him, but they got after me instead. Mad cause I found out their meetin' place. Moved they did, but they hain't left me alone to this day.

"They got them special Devil powers. They ease in your brain like a thought and torment your mind."

"Mrs. Press. I have a notation here from Jay's doctor at Broughton stating that Jay Press thought you were the cause of all his problems."

"Yeah, reckon that's right. He allus had to have somebody to blame things on. Never could take nothin on his own self. He had to blame everything on me. Why, when he had a case of the farts he claimed it was my cookin."

The jurors nor the crowd make a sound.

"Do you keep in touch with your four daughters?"

"I call 'em every single day, those that are close and don't cost nothin to call."

"Which daughter do you talk to most?"

"Mary, my oldest. Least ways I did afore this here thing happened. They won't let me talk to her no more. Just look at my baby girl sittin there. I oughta had more backbone."

"How old are you?"

"Me? Seventy-seven I reckon. Sometimes I forget, exactly."

"In my notes, Jay Press was evaluated in Broughton. It states he was obsessed by the need to control others."

Judge Kidd cleared his throat. "Mr. Mason, need I warn you this is not a trial about Jay Press."

"Please bear with me your honor. I do have an important point to conclude."

"Get on with it, then."

"Yes, your honor."

"Mrs. Press, in your opinion, would you say Jay Press was crazy?"

"I object. Mrs. Press is not qualified to answer that." Clawson didn't bother to stand up.

"I only ask her opinion. Certainly not as an expert witness. Only as a wife that lived with him."

"Mr. Mason, Mr. Clawson, would you please approach the bench."

Clawson got up and trudged forward in the mannerism that openly said that an easy case was being made extremely difficult by Mason.

"I want both of you to know I am giving a lot of leeway here. Now, get on with this trial. Mr. Mason, you better not be wasting the time of this court. As I stated before, Jay Press is dead and not on trial. The woman that shot him is."

"Yes, your honor. I think it is of dire importance for the jury to know what led up to that shooting."

Kidd's lips drew thin as he thought for a moment. "Mr. Mason, I'm going to let you continue with this line of questioning for reasons of my own." He looked at Clawson, and Clawson gave a tired look of consent.

Mason moved to the witness stand, trying his best not to smile with his victory. "Mrs. Press, in your opinion was Jay press crazy?"

"Crazy as a bed bug. That's why he was there in Morganton them times."

"In your opinion was Pete Press crazy?"

"Yeah, he was, but not as bad as Jay was."

"In your opinion is your daughter crazy?"

"No, she hain't."

"In your opinion are you crazy?"

"No I hain't, and you hain't got no right to say such a thing about me. I'm the sanest person I know of."

"No more questions, your honor."

"Do you wish to cross examine this witness, Mr. Clawson?"

Clawson was considering. He started to stand, hesitated, then stood.

"Yes, your honor." He moved slow, trudging toward her. "Mrs. Press, did you love your husband, Jay Press when you married him?"

She frowned, looked at Clawson hard. "I don't hardly know how to answer that one."

"Try answering it truthfully."

"I will have you that know I answer everthing truthfully."

"Did you love him?"

"As much as I knowd how."

"Do you not know how to love, Mrs. Press?"

"I certainly do. It's jest there hain't nobody a livin' what would know how to love Jay Press. I'm not sure his own mammy did, God rest her soul."

"Do you love your daughters?"

"I do."

"What mother who loved her daughters would leave them to a man as bad as you claim Jay Press to be?"

Ivy Press focused her faded blue eyes on him. Her face pinched up in anger. "A dead woman still able to walk."

Chapter 31

Harold Mason sat in his office looking over his notes for the Press/Tate trial. His assistants had provided excellent research for him. They had Jay Press's medical records from Broughton Hospital, and a list of his relatives back a hundred years.

He wasn't pleased. Reading the files left a knot of fear growing in the pit of his stomach. It expanded and filled his mind, making him look at his own wife, Anna, in a different light. A light filled with questions and fear.

He and Anna had gotten married by the magistrate. Anna had refused a formal wedding. She said she just wanted to be his wife without any fuss, bother, or expense. He didn't mind. He loved her and wanted her in his bed for the rest of his life.

Her parents now lived in Kinston, down below Raleigh. He had meet them a time or two. All he knew about them when he married Anna was that they were nice people.

He tried to put Anna from his mind as he thought about the case. The crowded courtroom had thinned out some from the first days. The newspaper wrote correct reports on what was happening without making big headlines. Judge Kidd was giving him free range with the trial, and Clawson didn't seem to care much. He tapped his pen on the folder a few times, ran his fingers through his hair.

Maybe he craved the excitement of city life. Maybe he wanted more than a quiet little country town had to offer. Maybe Anna would move to the city with him after the trial was over and everything came out. Although he feared what her answer would be, he would ask her again.

She loved the mountains. She loved the people. Why? He just didn't understand. She certainly saw something he had never seen. When he asked her, she said, "The people are real, Harold. They don't pretend at life. They don't pretend to be someone or something they are not. And Mason, they are my people."

He slowly reached for the phone and dialed the number written on the post-a-note his assistant left stuck to the folder

"Mrs. Johnson, do you suppose I could buy you dinner tonight?"

The woman that made her way to the witness stand had the crowd's attention. Diamond earrings sparkled in her ears. A gold necklace circled her throat. Her hair had been done the day before; it's color a pale, almost platinum blonde. Her face was smooth and her makeup was as perfect as time and money could make it. The clothes she wore could have a big sign on them reading 'expensive.'

Mrs. Ira Johnson took her seat on the witness stand, displaying the grace and dignity of a queen. Her voice was letter perfect when she said I do.

"Would you state your name please?" Harold Mason asked her.

"Mrs. Ira Johnson, Lacy Johnson."

"Mrs. Johnson, do you know the defendant, Mary Press Tate?"

"I knew her many years ago, when she was a baby."

"How old a baby?"

"Less than a year."

"Is there a reason you didn't know her beyond a year?"

"Yes."

"Would you care to state that reason?"

"Certainly. I moved away from the area."

"How long were you gone?"

"Almost sixty years."

"When did you move back?"

"Four months ago."

"Why did you move back four months ago?"

"My husband died and I came back home." She smiled, soft, gentle. "Returning to my roots, I guess. Strange, how you think you hate a place only to find mountain roots have grown into you heart. "

"Where do you reside?"

"I rent a place in Foscoe at present time."

"Are you having a home built?"

"Yes, sir."

"What is the name of the community?"

"It is my old home place. The community of Hemlock Ridge."

"What relationship is Jay Press to you?"

"He is my nephew."

The intake of breath filled the courtroom.

"What was your maiden name?"

"Lacy Dyke. I was the twelfth child of Zoe and Alvin Dyke."

"Would you tell in your own words how you left the mountains?"

"My sister Bobbie, who raised me since I was born, wanted a better life for me than she could provide. She asked Mattie Clark to take me under her wing and educate me."

"Mattie Clark agreed?"

"Yes, she did. I stayed at the Clark home until I went away to college. Bobbie allowed me to return home and visit on occasion, but she would not allow me to stay on Hemlock Ridge."

Were you ever alone on Hemlock Ridge?"

"I suppose I was, but I can't remember any particular occasion."

"Why is that?"

"Bobbie was always with me. She insisted I hold onto her hand or her dresstail while I was small. When I was older, she insisted I never get out of her sight."

"Do you know why Bobbie kept you in her sight?"

"Yes. She told me I was too pretty. She said there wasn't a man on Hemlock Ridge she would trust as far as she could throw a bull, unless it was our brother Clayton. She told me she did not save my life for it to be ruined on Hemlock Ridge."

"How old are you, Mrs. Johnson?"

"I am seventy-seven years old, almost seventy eight."

"According to my notes, you are not quite a year older than Ivy Press.

"That is correct."

"In all due respect to Ivy Press, you look much younger. How would you explain that?"   "My life has been easy. I married a man with gentle ways and gentle means. Poverty is devastating to a woman. It draws life out of her like a blown up balloon with a slow leak."

"Do you have any brothers or sisters living?"

"No. Dear Bobbie lived the longest of them all. Strange, being she was so small and frail." Lacy smiled. "To me, Bobbie was the lady of Hemlock Ridge."

"Bobbie was married to Reverend Hal Holloman. Is that correct?"

"Yes, she married Preacher Holloman."

"Mrs. Johnson, did you know Jay Press?"

"Yes."

"What type of man was he?"

"Pathetic to the point of disgusting," she said the words simply, matter of fact. No emotions came from her, just a repeated memory.

"Could you tell the jury why you feel that way?"

"Certainly. He reminded me of an animal, weasel I would say. He was always on the prowl trying to find things weaker than he was, as though torturing their weakness would make him stronger."

"By things, do you refer to people or animals?"

"Both. He preferred people."

"Was he afraid of anyone?"

"He was afraid of Clayton, my oldest brother. Clayton could make him behave. Unfortunately, for a lot of people on Hemlock Ridge, but to Clayton's benefit, Mr. Clark sent him away to school."

"What did Clayton do as a livelihood?"

"He taught agriculture at a State College."

"He did well for himself?"

"Himself, his wife, and four children."

Where do his children live?"

"The last Bobbie told me, Clayton never visited Hemlock Ridge. I don't know where all his children live."

Harold Mason never asked her if she knew that one of Clayton's daughters had moved back to the mountains for a while. He never asked her if one of Clayton Dyke's granddaughters was Anna Lee Taylor Mason, his wife. Instead, he continued his questioning in a different direction.

"Was there anyone else Jay feared?"

"He was afraid of Bobbie."

"You mean to tell me a big, tough man like Jay Press was afraid of a frail, little woman like Bobbie Holloman?"

"He wasn't afraid of her strength. He was afraid of her mind, the knowledge she obtained. I have often thought Bobbie being a preacher's wife might have added to it. Jay was mortified of God. He thought he had the Devil on his side, therefore he was determined to beat God."

Clawson didn't bother to stand. "I object your honor. She is speculating."

"Normally I would sustain that, however, I would like to know a little more about Jay Press, speculation or not. Overruled. Continue Mrs. Johnson."

"Jay was superstitious, claimed he could talk in tongues. I was with Bobbie when we heard this sound. We found Jay standing on a log preaching hell fire and brimstone. He was only eight or nine years old."

"What happened?

"He jumped off the log, grabbed a rock and hit Bobbie with it, then ran off. Bobbie told me to make sure I was never alone with him. She said he needed more help than all the people on Hemlock Ridge could give. It wasn't long after that, she sent me to live with Mattie Clark."

"Did Bobbie ever tell you why she sent you away?"

"I told you before. She wanted a better life for me. She knew I would suffer if I stayed there."

"Mrs. Johnson, I believe she told you more than that, didn't she?"

"She told me dirty laundry did not need to be washed in public."

"When a person's life is on trial, dirty laundry does not come into the equation. The truth must be told. Again, Mrs. Johnson, did Bobbie tell you more than that?"

"Yes."

"When?"

"It was about a year before she died. I knew she was in bad health, so I hired Delbert Hodges to drive her to my home. I had her sent to the doctor for a complete physical." She stopped talking and took a deep breath. No one noticed that her hands were gripped so tight her knuckles had turned white.

"What were the results of the physical?"

"She had a short time to live. She had been sick for many years. The doctor told me he did not know how she managed to stay alive for the last ten years. Cancer had penetrated most all of her internal organs. He also told me that her mind was clear and functioning normally."

"In other words she was not mentally impaired?"

"That is correct."

"Did Bobbie know she was dying?"

"Yes. She did."

"Was there a reason she refused to give in to cancer and let herself pass on?"

"Yes. "

"Would you please tell us why?"

"Because of her daughter."

"How many children did Bobbie have?"

"Just the one daughter." Lacy Johnson grinned. "Preacher Holloman was devastated. He wanted a son, a son granted by God in Preacher Holloman's own image."

"Mrs. Johnson, in your own words, can you tell us why Bobbie was concerned about leaving her daughter?"

"Her daughter had never been normal. It was obvious something was wrong with her since birth."

"Could you describe her daughter to us?"

"Physically she was all right. She was pretty and she ran and played like other children. It was her mind that worried Bobbie. She would have strange thoughts in her little mind. She would see things that were not there. Say things to Bobbie that made no sense at all. She was always slipping away from Bobbie and running through the woods. Bobbie would find her bed empty any time during the night, and find her outside wandering around in circles. Bobbie tried to get her help through Mattie Clark, but Mattie refused to take her in like she did me. Mattie was too old to look after such a difficult child, but she had a specialist check her."

"And," Mason encouraged. "What did this specialist say?"

"That she had mental problems."

"The cause of these problems?"

"He said it could be heredity or maybe even environment in the possibility she might have ingested something such as lead."

"Did you have any speculations at that time what could be wrong with the child?"

"No. Not at that time."

"Do you at this time?"

"Yes, of course I do."

"Mrs. Johnson, I am asking you to tell the jury your opinion. I repeat, your opinion of her problem."

"I believe most of it was heredity. Just as Jay Press's problem was heredity."

"Heredity in Jay Press because of his father, Pete Press?" Mason asked her.

"Yes, and because of my and Alva's own father. You see Pap was an alcoholic. I don't believe he ever had a sober moment in his adult life. And Maw, she would take spells where she would go blank. Maw, from what I've read, was schizophrenic. Maw had a world of problems and the fact that my father contaminated his sperm with alcohol left us children with a high probability of mental problems. To be completely truthful, I think each one of us children were affected."

"You appear normal."

She smiled. "I'm not."

"Mrs. Johnson, could we get back to Bobbie's daughter?"

"If we must."

"I think we must. It is imperative to this case. Can you tell us what happened to Bobbie's daughter?"

"What happened? She got married if that is what you're asking."

"How old was she when she got married?"

"Fifteen."

"Isn't fifteen young for marrying age?"

"Not at that period in time. Most all of the women in Hemlock Ridge community got married around that age."

"Did she get married with Bobbie's blessing?"

"Oh no! Bobbie wás devastated. She cried for days without stopping. She cried whenever she started thinking about it. She never stopped suffering over that marriage."

"Why didn't Bobbie forbid the marriage if she didn't approve?"

"They slipped off and got married. Bobbie hunted for hours when she found her gone. Bobbie thought she had just run off during one of her spells. She never expected marriage. You see, every person knew the girl wasn't mentally right. No one would court her, much less want to marry her."

"Yet, someone did?"

"Yes. Jay Press did. Married her just to spite Bobbie."

Harold Mason stopped his movements and looked at Lacy in disbelief. He turned toward the jury then back to Lacy. He lifted his hands, palms up, as though expressing his disbelief.

"You are telling this jury that Jay Press married his first cousin?"

"Yes."

"You are telling us that your family had a history of mental problems and Jay Press increased the chance of his own children having mental problems by marrying his first cousin? He did this just to spite Bobbie, the aunt he was afraid of?"

"Yes, sir. I think that is true."

"Mrs. Johnson, Lacy, is there more truth than you have told us?"

"Yes."

"Would you tell us the rest of the story now?"

"I would prefer not to." She looked at Mary. "I'm sorry, dear, but it may be time the truth is known for your own sake."

Mary looked at Lacy and shook her head as though she guessed what Lacy was going to tell. Lacy tried to smile and failed.

"Ivy was not only Jay Press's first cousin, she was his aunt. Pap raped Bobbie."

"No! No!" Ivy screamed from the back of the room. "I hain't no Dyke. I'm a Holloman. I'm a preacher's daughter!"

The tiny woman bolted from her seat and headed down the aisle toward Lacy. "You in your fancy getup, a sittin there a lyin' bout me! It's lies! All lies!"

Judge Kidd banged his gavel. "Remove her from this room."

A deputy caught her, lifted her feet off the floor, and took her from the room while kicking and screaming at the top of her lungs.

"This court is adjourned until tomorrow morning at nine o'clock."

Mason had his third stiff drink in a row, enough to make him restless and insistent. He got his wife Anna behind the wheel of his car and had her start driving.

"Harold, why are you doing this? It serves no purpose," Anna said.

"It does to me,"

"What? Just tell me what purpose?"

"I need to see Hemlock Ridge."

"No you don't. You've driven that road before, many times."

"It's been a long time back."

"Harold, you know you're just feeling guilty because of the uproar you caused today."

"Uproar? I caused?"

"That's what I just said. You caused an uproar."

"I had to do it. I'm sorry, Anna, but I had to do it."

"I've told you a dozen times, it's all right. I understand."

"But…"

"Harold, will you stop beating yourself up over this. People don't care who your wife is related to. Beside, I know what you're thinking. You're afraid that my being related to the Dykes will affect me or our children. It's just life Harold. We all have relatives. Some of them are going to be crazy and some will be super intelligent. It's just life, Harold."

She drove the car along a road that had recently been widened and paved. Only a few remaining shacks stood leaning in odd directions, pulled by gravity and rot, as reminder of a time that once was. A tiny rock building still stood next to a summer home. A doctor lived in the summer home a few weeks a year. He kept the rock building because he thought it quaint, never once knowing a woman named Alva proved she could build herself a house out of rocks.

Houses were built of grand proportions. Houses the likes of which no one ever thought would hang on a rocky mountain-side. Hemlock Ridge was no longer shut off from the world, drying up in poverty. Outsiders came into the mountains and brought money with them. A commodity that was once non-existent.

The mountain people were no longer isolated by the towering mountains that enclosed them.

Outsiders were coming fast and bringing money with them. They had moved to a place that was almost perfect, and then they set in to changing it with speed.

"Harold, you know that things are different now," she insisted.

He wondered just how different?

Chapter 32

Mason held Mary's trembling hand as they watched the jurors walk into the courtroom, single file, taking their seats in the jury box.

"It will be all right," Mason told her. "They came to a verdict fast. That's in your favor." He hoped.

Mary closed her eyes.

Mason stared at the piece of paper held in the foreman's hand. The paper that would tell him how good a job he had done with Mary's life.

Kidd looked at Mary. "Will the defendant please rise."

Mason thought he could hear her bones rattling as she made herself stand. She had to lean her weight against the table and hold the chair back with her hand to remain upright. Could there be a more terrifying moment in a person's life? That piece of paper contained the answer to her life, forever after.

"Mr. Forman would you please read the verdict," Judge Kidd said.

He unfolded the piece of paper, looked at it a moment, looked up at Judge Kidd then back at the paper.

"Not guilty by reason of insanity."

Noise filled the courtroom. Mary sank into her chair and began to cry.

"I'm free," she said. "Oh, thank God. I'm free."

Judge Kidd allowed the chaos for another minute then banged his gavel loud and clear. "Order in this courtroom." He demanded. "Order, order in the courtroom."

Mason put his arm around Mary and whispered in her ear. She quieted down, wiped her tear-streaked face, and looked at the judge, smiling.

"Mrs. Mary Tate, you have been tried by a jury of your peers and found not guilty by reason of insanity. It remains my duty to determine the extent of your insanity, and the consequences thereof. For your benefit, Mrs. Tate, I am sentencing you to Broughton Mental Hospital in Morganton, North Carolina, for the period of two years. At the end of such time, you will be evaluated to determine the need of further treatment."

Mason heard Kidd's words. Felt his mouth drop open. He had won the case and still he had lost it. Judge Kidd gave her the same sentence he always intended to give.

Yet, could he disagree?

He could file an appeal. He could demand time already served be subtracted from the two years, but should he?

Chapter 33

Mary Press Tate drove the little black Honda Civic up the gravel road, all the way up Tamarack. She listened to the rattles and the groan of the engine. She hadn't had enough money to buy much of a car, didn't want to buy much of one.

She had used part of her money to buy an acre of land from Lacy. She would use another part to buy her a used single-wide mobile home to set on the land.

She felt an aggravation twist inside her. Lacy could have afforded to give her an acre of land, that way she could buy herself a double wide. Better yet, Lacy could have let her live in that fancy house with her.

That old woman didn't need a big house like that when she was all alone. No, it wouldn't have hurt Lacy none. It would have helped her a plenty. She was tired of mobile homes, but, oh well, come time.

She stopped the car in the road, in front of where Pa's house used to stand. It was gone now, gone along with the stands of bees.

They had gotten a high price from the sale of the bees. Folks knew strange old men that raised bees hid their money inside bee gums.

Mary grinned. She guessed somebody was disappointed. She wasn't. She got a portion of the money from sale of the bees and sale of the land. That was how she afforded to buy her car, land, and mobile home.

Soon, there would be a big, fancy house sitting where her Pa's shack once stood. She wondered if another little child would have a hellhole like she had? She wondered if rich folks' kids ever got abused?

She walked over where the house used to be. It was cleared ground now, bulldozed off smooth as her hand, all the trash gone to the dump. She laughed out loud. Her trash was gone, too. According to the law, Broughton had worked for two years, three months and four days to bulldoze all of her trash away.

Doctor Alredd told the judge she was now in touch with reality. She was calm, cooperative, and compliant. He told the Judge she had a high IQ and could function on her own without threat to others or herself. In other words, she had done exactly what Alredd said the minute he wanted her to do it.

Funny, you were crazy if you did what you wanted, but sane if you did what somebody else wanted. Especially if that someone was in a position of authority.

She smiled as she left the housesite and walked down to the creek. She was never going back to that place in Morganton again. She would never have need to. Broughton Hospital was for crazy people and she was a long way from crazy.

She took off her shoes and waded in the cold water until her teeth began to chatter. She left the creek and went to the top of the rise where she could hear if a car was coming up Tamarack road. She heard nothing.

For a long time after she was released from that place, the sheriff, Big Red, had her followed. Once when she drove up here, he had stopped her at the bottom of the road and had a woman deputy search her and her car.

She made a habit of coming up here several times a week. She knew what harassment was. She knew the deputies could not stop her car and search without a reason. They knew she knew. She had complained to Mason.

She knew the value in patience. She knew there was a right and wrong time for everything.

She laughed.

Someday, she would have a big fancy house and plenty of money to live easy on, she wanted that and by God, she deserved it. Lacy was old. She wouldn't live much longer, and who was to say how much money Lacy left to her? Of course, she would see that Lacy left her the house. She had already figured that one out.

She walked through the woods as though she was wandering at random. She came to the large oak tree, the one Pa took her to often, one of the very spots where he wanted his crazy, abusive sex with a helpless child. She sat down at its roots and sat there listening, thinking. She was in no hurry. She had learned to wait her time.

When the woods became dark with dusk, she let her hand dig beneath a root in that special spot. Sure enough, it was there. Her glass jar. She twisted the rusty lid off, took out the money and stuck it beneath her dress next to the heat of her body.

She had made herself a sanitary pad, hollowed out in the center, just the right hollow to stuff a wad of money, a big wad. What deputy would search a woman's sanitary pad, even if she were in her sixties?

She went to the creek and washed her hands.

Big Red could have known what she did, if he had been a beekeeper and examined her hands that time he first arrested her. Bees had stung her hands when she took the money from the gums.

She had found Pa's protective suit, but not his gloves. She had taken her dress off, put the suit on, gotten the money and buried it, put her dress back on, then placed the suit in the house just like he had it. It was gone now, dumped in the trash with the rest of his things.

She had to dig her hands in the dirt so Big Red wouldn't see where the stings had left red, swollen places. There hadn't been many, but enough if a man had known bees.

She smiled and hummed a happy tune as she went back to her Honda Civic.

Mary knew that the sun shines on Tamarack Mountain, sometimes it shines while it rains.

If you enjoyed this book, visit peggypoestern.tripod.com to check on the status of Peggy's latest books or to leave feedback.

Books may be purchased regionally at selected stores in Northwestern North Carolina, Southwestern Virginia, and Eastern Tennessee.

To purchase online, visit appalachianauthorsguild.com or amazon.com.

For autographed copies, special print editions, or to contact author; e-mail, call, fax, or write:

Peggy Poe Stern
Moody Valley
475 Church Hollow Road
Boone, NC 28607
828-963-5331 Tel
828-963-4101 Fax
moodyvalley@skybest.com

Heaven High and Hell Deep

Laine's Beech Mountain Story

Peggy Poe Stern

Book 1, ISBN # 1-59513-055-1 $16.95

A mountain girl in the early 1900's copes with a marriage arranged by her dad. Her story is titled from an old saying "I own my land, heaven-high and hell-deep."

"Your pa gave his consent for us to marry," he said the words as though it was a simple matter. It wasn't a romantic proposal of love and devotion. It wasn't a proposal at all. I opened my mouth but nothing came out. I tried again.

"I don't know your name," I managed to say … .

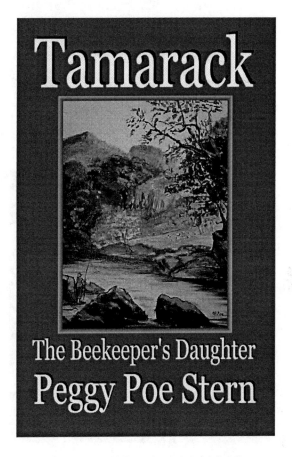

Tamarack

The Beekeeper's Daughter
Peggy Poe Stern

ISBN # 1-59513-054-3 $14.95

A gripping story about the dark side of a mountain family: a legacy of abuse that leads to murder. Told from an authentic mountain perspective, the reader experiences the family's desperation as well as their strength and determination to keep on going. The author's simple unabashed voice completely absorbs the reader. So many emotions are evoked that the story echoes long after the last page is read.

When Robins Weep

The Christmas Tree Lady
Peggy Poe Stern

ISBN # 1-59513-053-5 $17.95

A happenstance encounter between an Appalachian mountain girl and a Florida developer embarks them on a romantic relationship. Existing family ties coupled with completely diverse lifestyles complicate their love.

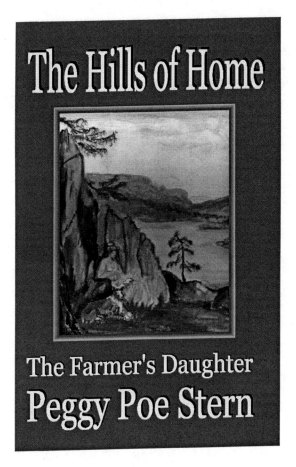

The Hills of Home

The Farmer's Daughter
Peggy Poe Stern

ISBN # 1-59513-052-7 $16.95

Theo Walden learns of love and understanding in her hills of home, plus a whole lot more. Granny teaches her that life isn't always fair or good. Greta fills her young head with ghost stories scary enough to keep her awake at night. Popaw and Daddy show her what its like to be mountain men: fair, tough, and yet gentle. Most important, Theo learns that wealth doesn't make a person happy. Love does.

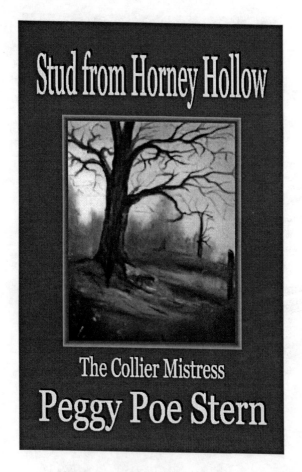

Stud from Horney Hollow

The Collier Mistress

Peggy Poe Stern

ISBN # 1-59513-051-9 $16.95

Willi Smith, a hard-nosed Florida real estate broker, had determined to get above her roots by obtaining wealth for the security it should bring. Having set her career before relationships, she realizes that her biological clock is ticking. She wants a child, but doesn't have a man.

Burl Horney, a widowed mountain Christmas tree grower, travels to Florida to sells his trees. Little does he know how he is being caught up in her quest.

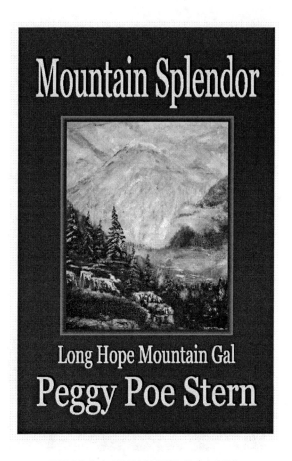

Mountain Splendor

Long Hope Mountain Gal
Peggy Poe Stern

ISBN # 1-59513-050-0 $16.95

Needing to make the farm payment, Ramona takes on her recently departed husband's next job assignment. Pretending to be a man, she guides a group of Yankees through the mountains. The tour is cut short, setting up a chain of events that keeps Ramona jumping from the frying pan to the fire.

Blood Moon Rising

Restless Revenge
Peggy Poe Stern

EAN # 978-1-59513-049-5 $16.95

The fires of hell would burn me in time for what I was about to do, but right now, that didn't matter. I was on my way to kill him. Someone should have killed Buck Walsh a long time ago for the things he did, but people were scared of him. I'm scared of him, but that no longer mattered either. He had raped me.

Wild Thing

Aggie's Legacy

Peggy Poe Stern

EAN #978-1-59513-048-8 $17.95

Cadence Williams settled beneath the quilt willing to go into a deep sleep. He hadn't slept much for the past two nights. Fear mixed with self-anger kept him awake. He hated fear. It was a sign of weakness, especially when it was his own. It angered him to fear when he wasn't sure if the cause of it was real or imagined. Yet, his gut told him *that thing* was near his house, moving in the woods like a dark shadow, stalking him when he went outside to do up the work, and even coming to his window during the night to watch him.

Above-all
a sequel to
Heaven-high and Hell-deep

Laine's Beech Mountain Story, Book 2
Peggy Poe Stern

EAN #978-1-59513-047-1 $17.00

His hat was pulled low over his black hair and his shirt sleeves were rolled up almost to his elbows. His hands appeared strong and in control as he held the reins of his high stepping horse. He looked a little thinner than he used to be and a lot more tired.

"What's wrong?" he asked me fast.

"You've got to go back to Banners Elk," I told him, forgetting about supper.

His eyes widened with concern. "Should you ride? I can deliver the baby here."

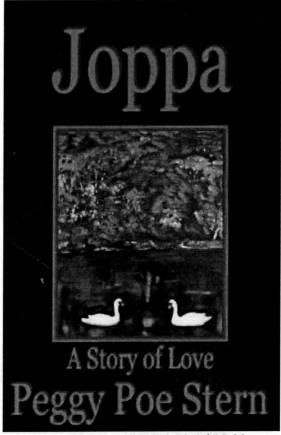

Joppa

A Story of Love
Peggy Poe Stern

EAN #978-1-59513-046-4 $17.00

"Leona," he sipped his hot coffee. "I know I'm going to regret asking this, but tell me the story of Joppa and Harry Barnard from the beginning to the end.

"It's a seventeen year stretch of time," I warned.

"This place isn't overrun with customers."

"If I tell you, will you use it against me. Claim I'm crazy; refuse to help me?"

"Attorney-client information is privileged. I don't tell anything you say not to tell."

"You'll think I'm a fruitcake."

"You're not?"